THE CANNIBAL ISLANDS

Capt Cook's Adventures in the South Seas

R.M. BALLANTYNE

Frontispiece by John Betancourt. Based on a painting.

THE CANNIBAL ISLANDS

Capt Cook's Adventures in the South Seas

R.M. Ballantyne

WILDSIDE PRESS

THE CANNIBAL ISLANDS

INTRODUCTION

Robert Michael Ballantyne (1825–1894) was a Scottish author who published more than 100 books. He was also an accomplished artist and exhibited some of his water-colours at the Royal Scottish Academy.

Ballantyne was born in Edinburgh, the ninth of ten children (and the youngest son), to Alexander and Anne Ballantyne. His father was a newspaper editor and printer in the family firm of "Ballantyne & Co" based at Paul's Works on the Canongate. His uncle, James Ballantyne, was the printer for Scottish author Sir Walter Scott. A banking crisis in 1825 resulted in the collapse of the Ballantyne printing business the following year with debts of £130,000,which led to a decline in the family's fortunes.

Robert Ballantyne went to Canada at the age of 16 and spent five years working for the Hudson's Bay Company. He traded with the local Native Americans for furs, which required him to travel by canoe and sleigh to the areas occupied by the modern-day provinces of Manitoba, Ontario, and Quebec—experiences that formed the basis of his novel *Snowflakes and Sunbeams* (1856). His longing for family and home during that period impressed him to start writing letters to his mother. Ballantyne recalled in his autobiographical *Personal Reminiscences in Book Making* (1893) that "To this long-letter writing I attribute whatever small amount of facility in composition I may have acquired."

In 1847 Ballantyne returned to Scotland to discover that his father had died. He published his first book the following year, *Hudson's Bay: or, Life in the Wilds of North America*, and for some time was employed by the publishers Messrs Constable. In 1856 he gave up business to focus on his literary career and began the series of adventure stories for the young with which his name is popularly associated.

The Young Fur-Traders (1856), *The Coral Island* (1857), *The World of Ice* (1859), *Ungava: a Tale of Eskimo Land* (1857), *The Dog*

Crusoe (1860), *The Lighthouse* (1865), *Fighting the Whales* (1866), *Deep Down* (1868), *The Pirate City* (1874), *Erling the Bold* (1869), *The Settler and the Savage* (1877), and more than 100 other books followed in regular succession, his rule being to write as far as possible from personal knowledge of the scenes he described. *The Gorilla Hunters: A tale of the wilds of Africa* (1861) shares three characters with The Coral Island: Jack Martin, Ralph Rover and Peterkin Gay. Here Ballantyne relied factually on Paul du Chaillu's Exploration in Equatorial Guinea, which had appeared early in the same year.

The Coral Island remains the most popular of the Ballantyne novels still read and remembered today, but because of a mistake he made in that book—he gave an incorrect thickness of coconut shells—he prioritized research on his subjects for later books. For instance, he spent time living with the lighthouse keepers at the Bell Rock before writing *The Lighthouse*, and he spent time with the tin miners of Cornwall while researching *Deep Down*.

In 1866 he married Jane Grant, with whom he had three sons and three daughters. He spent his later years in Harrow, London, before moving to Italy for the sake of his health, possibly suffering from undiagnosed Ménière's disease. He died in Rome in 1894 and was buried in the Protestant Cemetery there.

One of the young men influenced by Ballantyne's novels was Robert Louis Stevenson (1850–94). Stevenson was so impressed with the story of *The Coral Island* (1857) that he based portions of his most famous book, *Treasure Island* (1881), on themes found in Ballantyne's classic novel.

—Karl Wurf
Rockville, Maryland

CHAPTER I.

A Hero who rose from the Ranks.

More than a hundred years ago, there lived a man who dwelt in a mud cottage in the county of York; his name was Cook. He was a poor, honest labourer — a farm servant. This man was the father of that James Cook who lived to be a captain in the British Navy, and who, before he was killed, became one of the best and greatest navigators that ever spread his sails to the breeze and crossed the stormy sea.

Captain Cook was a true hero. His name is known throughout the whole world wherever books are read. He was born in the lowest condition of life, and raised himself to the highest point of fame. He was a self-taught man too. No large sums of money or long years of time were spent upon his schooling. No college education made him what he was. An old woman taught him his letters, but he was not sent to school till he was thirteen years of age. He remained only four years at the village school, where he learned a little writing and a little figuring. This was all he had to start with. The knowledge which he afterwards acquired, the great deeds that he performed, and the wonderful discoveries that he made, were all owing to the sound brain, the patient persevering spirit, the modest practical nature, and the good stout arm with which the Almighty had blessed him. It is the glory of England that many of her greatest men have risen from the ranks of those sons of toil who earn their daily bread in the sweat of their brow. Among all who have thus risen, few stand so high as Captain

Cook.

Many bold things he did, many strange regions he visited, in his voyages round the world, the records of which fill bulky volumes. In this little book we shall confine our attention to some of the interesting discoveries that were made by him among the romantic islands of the South Pacific — islands which are so beautiful that they have been aptly styled "gems of ocean," but which, nevertheless, are inhabited by savage races so thoroughly addicted to the terrible practice of eating human flesh, that we have thought fit to adopt the other, and not less appropriate, name of the Cannibal Islands.

Before proceeding with the narrative, let us glance briefly at the early career of Captain James Cook. He was born in 1728. After receiving the very slight education already referred to, he was bound apprentice to a shopkeeper. But the roving spirit within him soon caused him to break away from an occupation so uncongenial. He passed little more than a year behind the counter, and then, in 1746, went to sea.

Young Cook's first voyages were in connection with the coasting trade. He began his career in a collier trading between London and Newcastle. In a very short time it became evident that he would soon be a rising man. Promotion came rapidly. Little more than three years after the expiry of his apprenticeship he became mate of the *Friendship*, but, a few years later, he turned a longing eye on the navy — "having," as he himself said, "a mind to try his fortune that way." In the year 1755 he entered the King's service on board the *Eagle*, a sixty-gun ship, commanded by Sir Hugh Palliser. This officer was one of Cook's warmest friends through life.

In the navy the young sailor displayed the same steady, thorough-going character that had won him advancement in the coasting trade. The secret of his good fortune (if secret it may be called) was his untiring perseverance and energy in the pursuit of one object at one time. His attention was never divided. He seemed to have the power of giving his whole soul to the work in hand, whatever that might be, without troubling himself about the future. Whatever his hand found to do he did it with all his might. The consequence was that he became a first-rate man. His superiors soon found that out. He did not require to boast or push himself forward. His *work* spoke for him, and the result was that he was promoted from the forecastle to the quarter-deck, and became a master on board the *Mercury* when he was about thirty years of age.

About this time he went with the fleet to the Gulf of Saint Lawrence, and took part in the war then raging between the British and French in Canada. Winter in that region is long and bitterly cold. The gulfs and rivers there are at that season covered with thick ice; ships cannot move about, and war cannot be carried on. Thus the fleet was for a long period inactive. Cook took advantage of this leisure time to study mathematics and astronomy, and, although he little thought it, was thus fitting himself for the great work of discovery which he afterwards undertook with signal success.

In this expedition to Canada Cook distinguished himself greatly — especially in his surveys of the Gulf of Saint Lawrence, and in piloting the fleet safely through the dangerous shoals and rocks of that inland sea. So careful and correct was he in all that he did, that men in power and in high places began to take special notice of him; and, finally, when, in the year 1767, an expedition of importance was about to be sent to the southern seas for scientific purposes, Cook was chosen to command it.

This was indeed a high honour, for the success of that expedition depended on the man who should be placed at its head. In order to mark the importance of the command, and at the same time invest the commander with proper authority, Cook was promoted to the rank of lieutenant in the Royal Navy. He had long been a gentleman in heart and conduct; he was now raised to the social position of one by the King's commission.

From this point in his career Cook's history as a great navigator and discoverer began. We shall now follow him more closely in his brilliant course over the world of waters. He was about forty years of age at this time; modest and unassuming in manners and appearance; upwards of six feet high, and good-looking, with quick piercing eyes and brown hair, which latter he wore, according to the fashion of the time, tied behind in a pig-tail. It was not until the end of his first voyage that he was promoted to the rank of captain.

CHAPTER II.

Shows what Men will do and dare
in the Cause of Science.

Men who study the stars tell us strange and wonderful things — things that the unlearned find it hard to understand, and harder still to believe, yet things that we are now as sure of as we are of the fact that two and two make four!

There was a time when men said that the sun moved round the earth; and very natural it was in men to say so, for, to the eye of sense, it looks as if this were really the case. But those who study the stars have found out that the earth moves round the sun — a discovery which has been of the greatest importance to mankind — though the importance thereof cannot be fully understood except by scientific men.

Among other difficult things, these astronomers have attempted to measure the distance of the sun, moon, and stars from our earth. Moreover, they have tried to ascertain the exact size of these celestial lights, and they have, to a considerable extent, been successful in their efforts. By their complicated calculations, the men who study the stars can tell the exact day, hour, and minute when certain events will happen, such as an eclipse of the sun or of the moon.

Now, about the year 1768 the attention of the scientific world was eagerly turned to an event which was to take place in the following year. This was the passage of the planet Venus across the face of the sun. Astronomers term this the *Transit of*

Venus. It happens very seldom: it occurred in 1769, but not again till 1874, and 1882. By observing this passage – this transit – of Venus across the sun from different parts of our earth, it was hoped that such information could be obtained as would enable us to measure not only the distance of the sun from the earth with greater accuracy than heretofore, but also the extent of the whole host of stars that move with our earth around the sun and form what is called our Solar System.

An opportunity occurring so seldom was not to be lost. Learned men were sent to all parts of the world to observe the event. Among others, Captain Cook was sent to the south seas – there, among the far-off coral isles, to note the passage of a little star across the sun's face – an apparently trifling, though in reality important, event in the history of science.

So much for the object of Cook's first voyage. Let us now turn to the details thereof.

The vessel chosen by him for his long and dangerous voyage to unknown seas was a small one of only 370 tons burden. It was named the *Endeavour*. The crew consisted of forty-one seamen, twelve marines, and nine servants – these, with the officers and the scientific men of the expedition, made up a body of eighty-five persons.

The scientific men above mentioned were, Mr. Green, an astronomer; Mr. Banks, a naturalist, who afterwards became Sir Joseph Banks and a celebrated man; Doctor Solander, who was also a naturalist; and two draughtsmen, one of whom was skilled in drawing objects of natural history, the other in taking views of scenery.

The *Endeavour* was victualled for a cruise of eighteen months. She was a three-masted vessel of the barque rig, and carried twenty-two large guns, besides a store of small arms, – for the region of the world to which they were bound was inhabited by savages, against whom they might find it necessary to defend themselves.

When all was ready, Captain Cook hoisted his flag, and spread his sails, and, on the 26th of August 1768, the voyage began — England soon dropped out of sight astern, and ere long the blue sky above and the blue sea below were all that remained for the eyes of the navigators to rest upon.

It is a wonderful thought, when we come to consider it, the idea of *going to sea*! To sailors who are used to it, the thought, indeed, may be very commonplace, and to lazy minds that are not much given to think deeply upon any subject, the thought may not appear very wonderful; but it is so, nevertheless, to us, men of the land, when we calmly sit down and ponder the idea of making to ourselves a house of planks and beams of wood, launching it upon the sea, loading it with food and merchandise, setting up tall poles above its roof, spreading great sheets thereon, and then rushing out upon the troubled waters of the great deep, there, for days and nights, for weeks and months, and even years, to brave the fury of the winds and waves, with nothing between us and death except a wooden plank, some two or three inches thick!

It seems a bold thing for man to act in this fashion, even when he is accustomed to it, and when he knows all about the sea which he sails over; but when, like Cook, he knows very little about the far-off ocean to which he is bound, his boldness seems and really is, much greater. It is this very uncertainty, however, that charms the minds of enterprising men, and gives interest to such voyages.

The Bible says, "They that go down to the sea in ships, that do business in great waters; these see the works of the Lord, and His wonders in the deep." Navigators in all ages have borne testimony to the truth of this. The very first pages in Cook's journal mention some of these wonders. He says that, while they were off the coast of Spain, Mr. Banks and Dr. Solander, the naturalists, had an opportunity of observing some very curious marine animals, some of which were like jelly, and so colourless that it was difficult to see them in the water except at night, when they became luminous, and glowed like pale liquid fire. One, that was carefully examined, was about three inches long, and an inch thick, with a hollow passing quite through it, and a brown spot at one end, which was supposed to be its stomach. Four of these, when first taken up out of the sea in a bucket, were found to be adhering together, and were supposed to be one animal; but on being put into a glass of water they separated and swam briskly about. Many of them resembled precious stones, and shone in the water with bright and beautiful colours. One little animal of this kind lived several hours in a glass of salt water, swimming about with great agility, and at every motion displaying a change of colours.

These *Medusae*, as they are called, have been spoken of by many travellers, who tell us that in some parts of the sea they are so numerous that the whole ocean is covered with them, and seems to be composed of liquid fire, usually of a pale blue or green colour. The appearance is described as being of great splendour. Even in the seas on our own coasts this beautiful light is often seen. It is called phosphoric light. Something of the same kind may be seen in the carcass of a decaying fish if taken into a dark room.

Not long after this, they saw flying-fish. Cook says that when seen from the cabin windows they were beautiful beyond imagination, their sides having the colour and brightness of burnished silver. When seen from the deck they did not look so beautiful, because their backs were of a dark colour. It must not be supposed that these fish could fly about in the air like birds.

They can only fly a few yards at a time. They usually rise suddenly from the waves, fly as if in a great hurry, not more than a yard or two above the surface, and then drop as suddenly back into the sea as they rose out of it. The two fins near the shoulders of the fish are very long, so that they can be used as wings for these short flights. When chased by their enemy, the dolphin, flying-fish usually take a flight in order to escape. They do not, however, appear to be able to use their eyes when out of the water, for they have been seen to fly against ships at sea, get entangled in the rigging, and fall helpless on the deck. They are not quite so large as a herring, and are considered very good eating.

On drawing near to Cape Horn, on the extreme south of South America, the voyagers began to prepare for bad weather, for this Cape is notorious for its storms. Few mariners approach the Horn without some preparation, for many a good ship has gone to the bottom in the gales that blow there.

It was here that they first fell in with savages. The ship having approached close to that part of the land named Tierra del Fuego, natives were observed on shore. As Mr. Banks and Dr. Solander were anxious to visit them, a boat was lowered and sent ashore. They landed near a bay in the lee of some rocks where the water was smooth. Thirty or forty of the Indians soon made their appearance at the end of a sandy beach on the other side of the bay, but seeing that there were twelve Europeans in the boat they were afraid, and retreated. Mr. Banks and Dr. Solander then advanced about one hundred yards, on which two of the Indians returned, and, having advanced some paces, sat down. As soon as the gentlemen came up the savages rose and each threw away a small stick which he had carried in his hand. This was intended for a sign of peace. They then walked briskly towards their companions, who had halted about fifty yards behind them, and beckoned the gentlemen to follow, which they did. They were received with many uncouth signs of friendship, and, in return, gave the savages some beads and ribbons, which greatly delighted them.

A feeling of good-will having been thus established, the two parties joined and tried to hold converse by means of signs. Three of the Indians agreed to accompany them back to the ship, and when they got on board one of the wild visitors began to go through some extraordinary antics. When he was taken to any new part of the ship, or when he was shown any new thing, he shouted with all his force for some minutes, without directing his voice either to the people of the ship or to his companions.

Some beef and bread being given to them, they ate it, but did not seem to relish it much. Nevertheless, such of it as they did not eat they took away with them. But they would not swallow a drop either of wine or spirits. They put the glass to their lips, but, having tasted the liquor, they returned it with looks of disgust.

Cook says he was much surprised at the want of curiosity in these savages of the Cape, and seems to have formed a very low opinion of them. They were conducted all over the ship, yet, although they saw a vast number of beautiful and curious things that must have been quite new to them, they did not give vent to any expression of wonder or pleasure – for the howling above spoken of did not seem to be either, – and when they returned to land they did not seem anxious to tell what they had seen, neither did their comrades appear desirous of hearing anything about their visit to the ship. Altogether, they seemed a much lower race of people than the inhabitants of the South-Sea Islands whom Cook afterwards visited.

CHAPTER III.

*Describes an Adventure in the Mountains,
and tells of Tierra Del Fuego.*

One of the main objects that Mr. Banks and Dr. Solander had in view in going with Captain Cook on this voyage was to collect specimens of plants and insects in the new countries they were about to visit. The country near Cape Horn was at that time almost unknown: indeed, it is not much known even at the present day. The two naturalists of the expedition were therefore anxious to land and explore the shore.

Accordingly, early one fine morning a party went ashore to ascend one of the mountains. It consisted of Mr. Banks and Dr. Solander with their servants, two of whom were negroes; Mr. Buchan, the draughtsman; Mr. Monkhouse, the surgeon of the ship; and Mr. Green, the astronomer. These set off to push as far as they could into the country, intending to return before night. They were accompanied by two seamen, who carried their baggage.

The hills, when viewed from a distance, seemed to be partly wooded; above the wood there was a plain, and beyond that bare rocks. Mr. Banks hoped to get through the woods, and made no doubt that beyond it he would find new sorts of plants which no botanists had ever yet heard of. They entered the wood full of hope, and with much of the excitement that men cannot but feel when exploring a country that has never been trodden by the foot of a civilised man since the world began.

It took them, however, much longer to get through the pathless wood than they had expected. It was afternoon before they reached what they had taken for a plain, but which, to their great disappointment, they found to be a swamp covered with low bushes, which were so stubborn that they could not break through them, and were therefore compelled to step over them, while at every step they sank up to the ankles in mud — a mode of progress so fatiguing that they were all very soon exhausted. To make matters worse, the weather became gloomy and cold, with sudden blasts of piercing wind accompanied by snow.

They pushed on vigorously notwithstanding, and had wellnigh crossed the swamp when Mr. Buchan was suddenly seized with a fit. This compelled a halt. As he could not go further, a fire was kindled, and those who were most fatigued were left behind to take care of him, while the rest continued to advance. At last they reached the summit of the mountain, and were rewarded for their toil by the botanical specimens discovered there. It was late in the day by that time, and as it was impossible to get back to the ship that night, they were obliged to make up their minds to bivouac on the mountain, a necessity which caused them no little uneasiness, for it had now become bitterly cold. Sharp blasts of wind became so frequent, however, that they could not remain on the exposed mountain-side, and were obliged to make for the shelter of the woods in the nearest valley.

Mr. Buchan having recovered, and the whole party having reassembled, they set out to recross the swamp, intending, when they should get into the woods, to build a hut of leaves and branches, kindle a fire, and pass the night there as well as they could. But an overpowering torpor had now begun to seize hold upon some of the party, and it was with the greatest difficulty the others could prevent the drowsy ones from lying down to sleep in the snow. This almost irresistible tendency to sleep is common in cold countries. It is one of the effects of extreme cold upon exhausted men, and is a very dangerous condition, because those who fall into it cannot resist giving way to it, even though they know that if they do so they will certainly die.

Dr. Solander, who had formerly travelled on the snow-topped mountains of Norway, was aware of the danger of giving way to this feeling, and strove to prevent his companions from falling into the fatal rest. "Whoever sits down," said he, "will sleep, and whoever sleeps will awake no more."

Strange to say, Dr. Solander was the first to disregard his own warning. While they were still pushing across the naked side of the mountain, the cold became suddenly so intense that it increased the effect they dreaded so much. The doctor found the desire to rest so irresistible that he insisted on being suffered to lie down. Mr. Banks tried to prevent him, but in vain. Down he lay upon the ground, covered though it was with snow, and all that his friends could do was to keep shaking him, and so prevent him from falling into the fatal sleep. At the same time one of the negro servants became affected in a similar manner. Mr. Banks, therefore, sent forward five of the company with orders to get a fire ready at the first convenient place they could find, while himself with four others remained with the doctor and the negro, whom partly by entreaty and partly by force, they roused up and brought on for some little distance. But when they had got through the greatest part of the swamp they both declared they could go no further. Again Mr. Banks tried to reason with the two unfortunate men, pointing out their extreme danger, and beseeching them to make an effort to advance. But all he could say had no effect.

When the negro was told that if he would not go on he must, in a short time, be frozen to death, he answered that he desired nothing but to be allowed to lie down and die. Dr.

Solander, on being told the same thing, replied that he was willing to go on but that he must *"first take some sleep,"* forgetting apparently that he had before told his comrades that to sleep was to perish.

As Mr. Banks and his companions could not carry them, there was no help for it — they were suffered to sit down, being partly supported by the bushes. In a few minutes they were both sound asleep. Providentially, just at that time, some of the people who had been sent forward returned with the welcome news that a fire had been lighted not more than a quarter of a mile off. Renewed attempts were therefore made to rouse the sleepers. But the negro was past help. Every effort failed to awaken him. With Dr. Solander they were more successful, yet, though he had not slept five minutes he had almost lost the use of his limbs, and the muscles were so shrunken that the shoes fell off his feet. Staggering and stumbling among the slush and snow, more dead than alive, he was half carried, half dragged by his comrades to the fire.

Meanwhile the other negro and a seaman were left in charge of the unfortunate black servant, with directions to stay by him and do what they could for him until help should be sent. The moment Dr. Solander was got to the fire, two of the strongest of the party who had been refreshed were sent back to bring in the negro. In half an hour, however, they had the mortification to see these two men return alone. They had been unable to find their comrades. This at first seemed unaccountable, but when it was discovered that the only bottle of rum belonging to the party was amissing, Mr. Banks thought it probable that it had been in the knapsack of one of the absent men, that by means of it the sleeping negro had been revived, that they had then tried to reach the fire without waiting for assistance, and so had lost themselves.

It was by this time quite dark, another heavy fall of snow had come on, and continued for two hours, so that all hope of seeing them again alive was given up, for it must be remembered that the men remaining by the fire were so thoroughly knocked up that had they gone out to try to save their comrades they would in all probability have lost their own lives. Towards midnight, however, a shout was heard at some distance. Mr. Banks, with four others, went out immediately, and found the seaman who had been left with the two negroes, staggering along with just strength enough to keep on his legs. He was quickly brought to the fire, and, having described where the other two were, Mr. Banks proceeded in search of them. They were soon found. The first negro, who had sunk down at the same time with Dr. Solander, was found standing on his legs, but unable to move. The other negro was lying on the snow as insensible as a stone.

All hands were now called from the fire, and an attempt was made to carry them to it, but every man was so weak from cold, hunger, and fatigue that the united strength of the whole party was not sufficient for this. The night was extremely dark, the snow was very deep, and although they were but a short distance from the fire, it was as much as each man could do to make his way back to it, stumbling and falling as he went through bogs and bushes.

Thus the poor negroes were left to their sad fate, and some of the others were so near sharing that fate with them that they began to lose their sense of feeling. One of Mr. Banks's servants became so ill, that it was feared he would die before he could be got to the fire.

At the fire, however, they did eventually arrive, and beside it passed a dreadful night of anxiety, grief, and suffering. Of the twelve who had set out on this unfortunate expedition in health and good spirits two were dead; a third was so ill that it was doubtful whether he would be able to go forward in the morning; and a fourth, Mr. Buchan, was in danger of a return of his fits. They were distant from the ship a long day's journey, while snow lay deep on the ground and still continued to fall. Moreover, as they had not expected to be out so long, they had no provisions left, except a vulture which chanced to be shot, and which was not large enough to afford each of them quarter of a meal.

When morning dawned nothing was to be seen, as far as the eye could reach, but snow, which seemed to lie as thick upon the trees as on the ground, and the wind came down in such sudden violent blasts, that they did not dare to resume their journey. How long this might last they knew not. Despair crept slowly over them, and they began gloomily to believe that they were doomed to perish of hunger and cold in that dreary waste. But the Almighty, who often affords help to man when his case seems most hopeless and desperate, sent deliverance in a way most agreeable and unexpected. He caused a soft, mild breeze to blow, under the influence of which the clouds began to clear away, the intense cold moderated, and the gladdening sun broke forth, so that with revived spirits and frames the wanderers were enabled to start on the return journey to the coast.

Before doing so, they cooked and ate the vulture, and it is probable that they devoured that meal with fully as much eagerness and satisfaction as the ravenous bird itself ever devoured its prey. It was but a light breakfast, however. After being skinned, the bird was divided into ten portions, and every man cooked his own as he thought fit, but each did not receive above three mouthfuls. Nevertheless it strengthened them enough to enable them to return to the ship, where they were received by their anxious friends with much joy and thankfulness.

The month of December is the middle of summer in the land at the extreme south of South America.

That land occupies much about the same position on the southern half of this world that we occupy on the northern half; so that, when it is winter with us, it is summer there. The climate is rigorous and stormy in the extreme, and the description given of the natives shows that they are a wretched and forlorn race of human beings. Captain Cook visited one of their villages before leaving the coast. It contained about a dozen dwellings of the poorest description. They were mere hovels; nothing more than a few poles set up in a circle and meeting together at the top, each forming a kind of cone. On the weather side each cone was covered with a few boughs and a little grass. The other side was left open to let the light in and the smoke out. Furniture they had none. A little grass on the floor served for chairs, tables, and beds. The only articles of manufacture to be seen among the people were a few rude baskets, and a sort of sack in which they carried the shell-fish which formed part of their food. They had also bows and arrows, which were rather neatly made — the arrows with flint heads cleverly fitted on.

The colour of those savages resembled iron-rust mixed with oil; their hair was long and black. The men were large but clumsy fellows, varying from five feet eight to five feet ten. The women were much smaller, few being above five feet. Their costume consisted of skins of wild animals. The women tied their fur cloaks about the waists with a thong of leather. One would imagine that among people so poor and miserably off there was not temptation to vain show, nevertheless they were fond of making themselves "look fine"! They painted their faces with various colours; white round the eyes, with stripes of red and black across the cheeks, but scarcely any two of them were painted alike. Both men and women wore bracelets of beads made of shells and bones, and, of course, they were greatly delighted with the beads which their visitors presented to them. Their language was harsh in sound; they seemed to have no form of government, and no sort of religion. Altogether they appeared to be the most destitute, as well as the most stupid, of all human beings.

CHAPTER IV.

Explains how Coral Islands are made.

Soon after this adventurous visit to the land of Tierra del Fuego, the *Endeavour* doubled Cape Horn — and entered the waters of the great Pacific Ocean; and now Cook began to traverse those unknown seas in which his fame as a discoverer was destined to be made. He sailed over this ocean for several weeks, however, before discovering any land. It was on Tuesday morning, the 10th of April, that he fell in with the first of the coral islands. Mr. Banks's servant, Peter Briscoe, was the first to see it, bearing south, at the distance of about ten or twelve miles, and the ship was immediately run in that direction. It was found to be an island of an oval form, with a lake, or lagoon, in the middle of it. In fact, it was like an irregularly-formed ring of land, with the ocean outside and a lake inside. Coral islands vary a good deal in form and size, but the above description is true of many of them.

To this island the crew of the *Endeavour* now drew near with looks of eager interest, as may well be believed, for an unknown land necessarily excites feelings of lively curiosity in the breasts of those who discover it.

It was found to be very narrow in some places, and very low, almost on a level with the sea. Some parts were bare and rocky; others were covered with vegetation, while in several places there were clumps of trees — chiefly cocoa-nut palms. When the ship came within a mile of the breakers, the lead was hove, but no bottom was found with 130 fathoms of line! This was an extraordinary depth so near shore, but they afterwards found that most of the coral islands have great depth of water round them, close outside the breakers.

They now observed that the island was inhabited, and with the glass counted four-and-twenty natives walking on the beach. These all seemed to be quite naked. They were of a brown colour, and had long black hair. They carried spears of great length in their hands, also a smaller weapon, which appeared to be either a club or a paddle. The huts of these people were under the shade of some palm-trees, and Captain Cook says that to him and his men, who had seen nothing but water and sky for many long months, except the dreary shores of Tierra del Fuego, these groves appeared like paradise.

They called this Lagoon Island. As night came on soon after they reached it, however, they were compelled to sail away without attempting to land.

Not long afterwards another island was discovered. This one was in the shape of a bow, with the calm lake, or lagoon, lying between the cord and the bow. It was also inhabited, but Cook did not think it worth his while to land. The natives here had canoes, and the voyagers waited to give them an opportunity of putting off to the ship, but they seemed afraid to do so.

Now, good reader, you must know that these coral islands of the Pacific are not composed of ordinary rocks, like most other islands of the world, but are literally manufactured or built by millions of extremely small insects which merit particular notice. Let us examine this process of island-making which is carried on very extensively by the artisans of the great South-Sea Factory!

The coral insect is a small creature of the sea which has been gifted with the power of "secreting" or depositing a lime-like substance, with which it builds to itself a little cell or habitation. It fastens this house to a rock at the bottom of the sea. Like many other creatures the coral insect is sociable; it is fond of company, and is never found working except in connection with millions of its friends. Of all the creatures of earth it shows perhaps the best example of what mighty works can be accomplished by *union*. One man can do comparatively little, but hundreds of men, united in their work, can achieve wonders, as every one knows. They can erect palaces and cathedrals towering to the skies; they can cover hundred of miles of ground with cities, and connect continents with telegraphs, but, with all their union, all their wisdom, and all their power, men cannot build islands – yet this is done by the coral insect; a thing without hand or brain, a creature with little more than a body and a stomach. It is not much bigger than a pin-head, yet hundreds of the lovely, fertile islands of the Pacific Ocean are formed by this busy animalcule. Many of those islands would never have been there but for the coral insect!

When corallines (as they are called) set about building an island, they lay the foundation on the top of a submarine mountain. The ordinary islands of the sea are neither more nor less than the tops of those mountains which rise from the bottom of the sea and project above the surface. Some of these sea-mountains rise high above the surface and form large islands; some only peep, so to speak, out of the waves, thus forming small islands; others again do not rise to the surface at all – their highest peaks being several feet below the level of the ocean. It is on these water-covered mountain-tops that the coral insects lay the foundations of their islands. As few mountain-peaks are level, however, whether above or below water, the insect finds it more convenient to form a ring round the sides of the mountain-top than to build on the exact top itself. Then they set to work with the busy industry of bees. Their talents are few; apparently they have received only one, but they turn that one to good account. They fulfil the work for which they were created. No creature can do more!

They begin to build, and the work advances rapidly, for they are active little masons. The ring round the mountain-top soon begins to shoot upwards and extend outwards. As the labourers continue their work their families increase. It is a thriving and a united community. There are neither wars nor disputes – no quarrelling, no mis-spent time, no misapplied talents. There is unity of action and design, hence the work advances quickly, steadily, and well. In process of time the coral ring becomes a solid wall, which gradually rises above the highest peak of the submarine mountain, and at length approaches the surface of the sea. When it reaches this point the work is done. The coral insect can only work under water. When its delicate head rises above the waves it ceases to build, and, having done its duty, it dies. Those which reach the surface first, die first. The others that are still below water work on, widening and strengthening the wall until they too reach the fatal surface, peep for one moment as it were on the upper world and then perish. Thus the active builders go on adding to the width of the structure, and dying by successive relays; working with their little might during their brief existence, and knowing nothing of the great end which is to result from their modest busy lives.

With the death of the coral insects the foundation-stone of the island is laid, in the form of a ring just peeping out of the ocean. Thenceforth other creatures continue the work. The waves lash and beat upon the uppermost coral cells and break them up into fine white sand. Currents of ocean throw upon this beach pieces of sea-weed and drifting marine substances of various kinds. The winds convey the lighter seeds of land plants to it, and sea-birds that alight upon it to rest do the same thing. Thus, little by little, things accumulate on the top of the coral ring until the summit rises above the reach and fury of the waves. No sooner is this accomplished than the genial sun of those regions calls the seeds into life. A few blades of green shoot up. These are the little tokens of life that give promise of the luxuriance yet to come. Soon the island ring is clothed with rich and beautiful vegetation, cocoa-nut palms begin to sprout and sea-fowl to find shelter where, in former days, the waves of the salt sea alone were to be found. In process of time the roving South-Sea islanders discover this little gem of ocean, and take up their abode on it; and when such a man as Cook sails past it, he sees, perchance, the naked savage on the beach gazing in wonder at his "big canoe," and the little children swimming like ducks in the calm waters of the lagoon or gambolling like porpoises among the huge breakers outside that roll like driven snow upon the strand.

During their formation, these islands are fraught with danger to ships, for sometimes, in parts of the ocean where charts show deep water, the sailor finds an unexpected coral reef, and, before he is aware, the good ship runs on this living wall and becomes a wreck. Many a noble vessel goes to sea well appointed and with a good brave crew, but never more returns; — who knows how many such have, when all on board thought themselves secure, been dashed to pieces suddenly, and lost upon the coral reefs of the Pacific?

These circular islets of coral never rise more than a few feet above the surface of the sea, but there are many other islands in the South Seas — some of which have been thrown up by the action of volcanoes, and are wild, rugged, mountainous, and of every conceivable shape and size.

The busy corallines before mentioned are so numerous in the South Seas that they build their coral walls everywhere. As they have an objection apparently to commence building in shallow water, they are obliged to keep off the shore a distance of a mile or more, so that when they reach the surface they enclose a belt of water of that width, which is guarded by the reef from the violence of the waves, and forms a splendid natural harbour. Almost every South-Sea island has its coral reef round it, and its harbour of still water between the reef and the shore.

It would seem as if the beneficent Creator had purposely formed those harbours for man's convenience, because narrow openings are found in all the reefs, without which, of course, the sheltered waters within could not have been entered. These openings are usually found to occur opposite valleys where the streams from the mountains enter the sea. It is therefore supposed that fresh water kills the coral insects at these places, thus preventing the reef from forming an unbroken circle. Low islets are usually formed on each side of the openings on which a few cocoa-nut trees grow; so that the mariner is thus furnished with a natural beacon by which to guide his vessel clear of the reef safely into the harbour.

One of the most interesting of the larger islands of the Pacific is Otaheite (now spelt and pronounced Tahiti), at which Captain Cook arrived on the 4th of April 1769. It had been discovered, however, nearly two years before the date of his visit – as the next chapter will show.

CHAPTER V.

Discovery by Captain Wallis of Otaheite or Tahiti.

The beautiful island of Tahiti was discovered by Captain Wallis in the year 1767.

It was on a bright day in June when he first saw it from the deck, but when his vessel (the *Dolphin*) came close to it, a thick mist descended like a veil and shut it out from view of the impatient mariners, who were compelled to lie to until the mist should clear away. At length it rolled off, and disclosed one of the most lovely and delightful scenes that could be imagined.

The *Dolphin* being the first ship that ever touched at Tahiti, the natives, as we may well imagine, were filled with amazement at its vast size and curious shape. No sooner did the ship draw near than she was surrounded by hundreds of canoes, containing altogether nearly a thousand naked savages. At first the poor creatures were afraid to draw near. They sat in their little barks gazing at the "big canoe" in silent wonder or talking to each other about her in low eager tones, but never for a moment taking their eyes off this great sight!

At last, after consulting together, they began to paddle slowly round the ship, and make signs of peace and friendship, which those on board were not slow to return, endeavouring to induce some of them to come on deck. This they were naturally afraid to do, but at length one fellow took heart and began by making a speech, which lasted for full fifteen minutes. As none of the sailors understood a word of it, they were not much enlightened; but the savage, who held a branch of the plantain-tree in his hand during his oration, concluded by casting this branch into the sea. This was meant as a sign of friendship, for soon after, a number of similar branches were thrown on the ship's deck, and then a few of the islanders ventured on board.

There was "much talk," however, on the part of the savages, before they began to feel at ease. Trinkets of various kinds were now offered to them, and they gazed around them with great interest, gradually losing their fears under the kindness of Captain Wallis and his companions. This happy state of things, however, was suddenly interrupted by a goat belonging to the ship, which, not liking the appearance of the strangers, attacked one of them unceremoniously, and butted at him with its head. Turning quickly round, the savage was filled with terror on beholding a creature, the like of which he had never seen before, reared on its hind legs, and preparing to repeat the blow. Without a moment's hesitation he rushed in consternation to the ship's side, and plunged into the sea, whither he was followed by all his countrymen in the twinkling of an eye. A storm of musket bullets could not have cleared the deck more quickly than did the attack of that pugnacious goat!

In a short time they recovered from their terrors, the ill-behaved goat was removed, and some of the natives were again induced to return on board, where they were treated with the utmost kindness, and presented with such trifling gifts as beads and nails, etc., much to their delight. Notwithstanding this, however, the visit terminated inharmoniously in consequence of one of the natives snatching a gold-laced hat from an officer's head, and jumping with it into the sea!

After this Wallis stood in-shore, intending to anchor, and sent his boats still closer to the land to take soundings. Here they were immediately surrounded by a great number of canoes, and the captain, suspecting the natives of hostile intentions, fired a nine-pounder over their heads. They were much startled by the unknown and terrible sound, but, seeing that no result followed, they proceeded to attack the boats, sending showers of stones into them, and wounding some of the men. It now became necessary to act in earnest, so a musket-shot was discharged at the savage who began the attack. The ball pierced his shoulder, whereupon the whole host paddled to the shore in great terror and confusion.

Notwithstanding this, the islanders soon returned to the ship with their boughs of peace: a speech was made by one of them. A few trinkets were given by the Europeans, and friendship was again restored; but next morning, when the boats were inshore searching for fresh water, a second attack was made upon them. Three large canoes ran against the ship's cutter, and stove in some of her upper planks. The natives were about to leap on board when a volley was fired into them, and two of their number fell into the sea. On seeing this they instantly retired, and the wounded men were dragged into the canoes.

Never having seen the effects of fire-arms before, the astonished savages apparently could not understand what was wrong with their comrades. They set them on their feet, but finding they could not stand, they tried to make them sit upright. One of them being only wounded, was able to remain in this position, but the other was dead, so they had to lay him in the bottom of their canoe. Once again they made peaceful signs, and Wallis, who was most anxious to avoid bloodshed, met them more than half-way. Traffic was speedily opened, and a considerable quantity of fruit, fowls, and hogs was obtained in exchange for scissors, knives, beads, and small trinkets of little value. But this did not last long. Warlike preparations were renewed by the natives, and many of their canoes were seen to be filled with large pebbles.

At last an attack was made on the ship itself, and a regular battle was fought.

This happened early in the morning when the sailors were engaged trafficking with the people in the canoes that contained provisions. Captain Wallis observed, with some anxiety, that, besides those provision canoes, many others of large size and filled with stones were gradually crowding round the ship; he therefore kept part of the crew armed, and loaded his guns. More canoes were putting off from shore and crowding round until there were about three hundred of them, with upwards of two thousand men, some of whom sang a gruff sort of war-song, while others blew into a shell as if it were a trumpet, and some played on an instrument resembling a flute.

In the midst of these discordant noises one canoe, larger than the others, and with a canopy over it, pushed alongside, and a naked warrior handed up a bunch of red and yellow feathers. This was, of course, supposed to be a sign of peace, but such was not the case. Immediately afterwards the canoe pushed off and the leader threw into the air the branch of a cocoa-nut tree. This was the signal. A general shout burst from the savages; the canoes made for the ship, and showers of stones were thrown on board. Many of these stones were fully two pounds weight, and as they were thrown with great force, some of the sailors were severely wounded.

The crew of the *Dolphin* rushed to quarters. The watch on deck instantly opened a fire of musketry on those nearest the ship, and two of the quarter-deck swivel guns, which happened to be loaded with small-shot, were also discharged. This warm and vigorous reception checked the attack for a few minutes; but the courage of the savages was aroused. They quickly renewed the assault, coming on in all directions, and receiving constant rein-forcements from the shore. But now the great guns of the ship were brought into play; the thunder of artillery echoed, for the first time, from the mountain-sides of Tahiti; and, as the heavy balls tore up the sea and crashed upon the shore, the terrified natives in the canoes nearest the ship took to flight.

Seeing this, the Captain at once ordered the fire to cease, being anxious to do as little harm as possible. This, however, had the effect of restoring confidence to the natives, who lay for some time gazing at the ship from a considerable distance. They had evidently profited by their short experience in this new style of warfare, for, observing that the terrible iron shower came thundering only from the *sides* of the ship, they made their next attack on the bow and stern — advancing with much daring, and throwing their stones with great violence and good aim, insomuch that some more of the men were severely hurt.

There is no saying what might have been the end of this fight, had not a lucky cannon-shot, fired from one of the great guns that had been run out at the bow, hit the canoe of the savage chief, and cut it in two. A result so tremendous had the effect of filling the hearts of the savages with terror. Every canoe turned tail and made for the shore in dire confusion, while the people who had crowded the beach took to their heels and ran over the hills in the utmost haste, as if they felt their only safety lay in placing the mountains between them and the terrible strangers in the big canoe. In half an hour not a single canoe was to be seen!

Captain Wallis now hoped that the natives would feel his immense superiority, and cease a useless contest, but he was mistaken. He was not yet done with them. They were a very determined set of men. Soon after this fight they were observed making preparations for a renewed attack. They could be seen pouring over the hills in all directions, and lurking in the thickets, while, round the point, numbers of war-canoes came paddling to the beach, where fresh warriors and bags of stones were embarked. It was evident that a grand attack was to be made; so Wallis prepared to repel it. Soon after, the bay was crowded with canoes as they paddled straight and swift toward the ship. At once the great guns opened with terrible effect, and so tremendous a fire was kept up that the entire flotilla was almost instantly dispersed. Many of the canoes were run ashore and deserted; others fled round the point, and the savages took to the woods. Into these the fire was then directed, and the natives, who doubtless imagined that no danger could penetrate from such a distance into the heart of their thick bushes, were driven, astonished and horrified, up a hill on which thousands of women and children had taken up their position to witness the fight.

Here they deemed themselves quite safe, but Captain Wallis resolved to show them that they were not so. He thought that the best thing he could do would be to inspire them with a wholesome dread of his tremendous artillery, so he ordered the guns to be fired at the crowded hill. The shots tore up the earth near a tree under which a dense crowd was collected. It need scarcely be added that the whole host fled on the wings of terror, and in less than two minutes not a man, woman, or child was to be seen.

The natives now at length submitted. Not many hours after the close of this fight, a few of them came down to the beach carrying green boughs which they stuck into the sand, and placed beside them a peace-offering of hogs and dogs and bundles of native cloth. Of course Wallis was right glad to accept it, and in return gave them presents of hatchets, nails, and other things. Peace was now thoroughly established, and the two parties engaged in amicable traffic with as much good-will as if they had neither quarrelled nor fought. The queen of the island visited the ship, and from that time till the *Dolphin* left everything went smoothly.

The ignorance of the natives as to the relative value of various metals was curiously shown one day. In order to find out what things they liked best, Captain Wallis spread before them a coin called a johannes, a guinea, a crown piece, a Spanish dollar, a few shillings, some new halfpence, and two large nails, and made a sign to them to help themselves. The nails were first seized with great eagerness, and then a few of the glittering new halfpence, but the silver and gold lay neglected!

The friendship thus established continued to increase as long as Wallis remained there, and when at length he took his departure the natives exhibited every sign of extreme regret – the queen especially was inconsolable, and wept bitterly when she bade them farewell.

Such were a few of the scenes that occurred at the discovery of Tahiti, an island which has since become famous as the scene of the residence of the mutineers of the *Bounty*, and the field of much earnest and deeply interesting missionary labour.

CHAPTER VI.

Captain Cook's Visit to Tahiti.

Less than two years after the discovery of Tahiti by Wallis, Captain Cook arrived in the *Endeavour* at the same island. He first saw its high mountains rise on the horizon on the 11th of June 1769, and soon afterwards a few canoes came off to the ship, but the natives were timid at first. They evidently had not forgotten the thundering guns and crashing shot of the *Dolphin*.

In every canoe there were young plantains and branches of trees, which latter were intended as tokens of peace and friendship. The people in one of the canoes ventured to the ship, and handed these branches up the side, making signals at the same time with great earnestness. At first the sailors were unable to make out their meaning, but at length, guessing that they wished those symbols to be placed in some conspicuous part of the ship, they immediately stuck them about the rigging, upon which the natives expressed the greatest satisfaction. Cook then purchased the cargoes of the canoes, consisting of cocoa-nuts and various kinds of fruits, which, after their long voyage, were most acceptable.

Next morning the *Endeavour* was safely anchored in a bay called by the natives Matavai. Here the visitors were received with much kindness. The natives regarded them with great respect and awe; the first man who approached them crouching so low that he almost crept on his hands and knees. Then two of the chiefs came forward, and each selected his friend. One chose Cook, and the other selected Mr. Banks, and each, taking off the greater part of his clothes, put them solemnly on his chosen friend.

On visiting their houses afterwards, they passed through delightful groves of trees which were loaded with cocoa-nuts and bread-fruit. These were found to be most excellent food. Before becoming quite ripe the liquid inside the cocoa-nut is said to resemble lemonade, when riper it is more like milk; and the bread-fruit nut, when properly dressed, is like the crumb of wheaten bread; so that it may be said of those favoured regions, with some degree of truth, that the people find something like bread and milk growing on the trees! There is indeed little occasion there for men to work. The fruits of the earth grow luxuriantly in a wild state; hence the natives, although a strong and active race, are habitually indolent. It has been proved, however, that when the blessed influence of the Christian religion is brought to bear on them, the South-Sea islanders are, in mind and body, good specimens of mankind.

One of the houses visited by Cook, in company with Messrs. Banks and Monkhouse, Dr. Solander and others, on his first landing, was that of Tootahah, a middle-aged man, who seemed to be a person of rank. He received them hospitably, spread mats for the party, desired them to sit down by his side, and gave them an excellent dinner of bread-fruit, cocoa-nuts, plantains, and fish – the latter raw as well as dressed. Cook naturally preferred his fish cooked, but the natives seemed to relish it raw! Thereafter Tootahah presented Mr. Banks and Captain Cook with a cock and hen, which curious gifts they accepted with many thanks, and in return gave Tootahah a laced silk neckcloth and a pocket handkerchief, in which he immediately dressed himself with immense satisfaction. Mr. Banks seems to have been a favourite with the savage ladies, for they plied him earnestly with cocoa-nut milk. He, as well as Cook, received a further gift of native cloth, which, although rough in texture, was agreeably perfumed.

Beads and other ornaments were presented to the women, and altogether the new friends were becoming mutually delighted with each other when a sudden interruption to the harmonious meeting was caused by the discovery that some of the savages had acquired the art of picking pockets. A snuff-box belonging to Mr. Monkhouse disappeared, and an opera-glass in a shagreen case, the property of Dr. Solander, vanished. To pass over a first act of this kind lightly would have led to interminable pilferings and quarrellings. Mr. Banks therefore started up angrily and struck the butt of his musket violently on the ground. Whereupon the most of the natives were panic-stricken, and darted out of the hut with the utmost precipitation. The chief endeavoured to appease the wrath of his guests by offering them gifts of cloth; but they were not thus to be silenced. They insisted on the restoration of the stolen articles, so the chief went out and shortly after returned with a beaming countenance – he had found them both; but his countenance fell when, on opening the case of the opera-glass, the glass itself was not there. With immense energy he resumed his detective duties, and was so fortunate as to recover the glass in a short time. Thus peace was restored, and the natives were taught to feel that their propensity to steal would prove a source of great annoyance and some danger to them, should they venture to give way to it in future.

Soon after this Cook selected a spot on the beach, not far from the ship, and, pitching his tent there, began to arrange for making the astronomical observations which had brought him to the South Seas. They had not remained long, however, before they found that the islanders were all addicted to stealing. Cook tells us that men and women of all ranks were the "arrantest thieves upon the face of the earth," yet they seemed to feel that the act of theft was wrong, for if charged with being guilty when they were in reality innocent, they were often moved to passionate indignation.

One day, when a large number of natives visited the ship, the chiefs employed themselves in stealing what they could in the cabin, while their dependants were no less industrious in other parts of the ship. They snatched up everything that it was possible for them to secrete till they got on shore. Two knives had been lost on shore, one of them belonging to Mr. Banks, who taxed a man named Tubourai Tamaide, whom he suspected, with the theft. The man denied it stoutly, but upon Mr. Banks saying firmly that, no matter who had taken it, he was determined to have it back, another native, feeling alarmed for his own safety, stepped forward and produced a rag in which three knives were tied up. One belonged to Dr. Solander, another to Captain Cook; the owner of the third was not known. Mr. Banks continued to charge Tubourai Tamaide with the theft of his knife, and the poor man continued to deny it indignantly. Not long after, it was discovered to have been mislaid by Mr. Banks's own servant, who at length found it. Upon this demonstration of his innocence, Tubourai expressed strong emotions of mind. The fellow was, doubtless, as great a thief as the rest of his comrades, but on this occasion he felt himself to be an injured innocent, and refused to be comforted until Mr. Banks expressed great sorrow for his unjust accusation, and made him a few trifling presents, whereupon he immediately forgot his wrongs and was perfectly reconciled!

In his dealings with these natives Captain Cook invariably acted with the gentleness, firmness, and wisdom of a truly great man, and at all times treated evil-doers with impartial justice.

One day a chief came to the tent on the beach in a state of intense excitement, and, hastily seizing Mr. Banks by the arm, made signs that he should follow him. Mr. Banks immediately complied, and soon came to a place where they found the ship's butcher with a reaping-hook in his hand. Here the chief stopped, and in a transport of rage explained, as well as he could by signs, that the butcher had threatened to cut his wife's throat with the hook. Mr. Banks assured him that, if he could fully explain the offence, the man should be punished. Upon this he became calm, and explained that the offender, having taken a fancy to a stone hatchet which lay in his house, had offered to purchase it of his wife for a nail; that she having refused to part with it, he had seized it, and, throwing down the nail, threatened to cut her throat if she made any resistance. As the nail and hatchet were produced in proof of this charge, and the butcher had little to say in his defence, there was no reason to doubt its truth.

On the matter being reported to Cook, he took the opportunity of the chief and his wives with a number of natives being on board the ship, to call up the butcher, and, after repeating the charge and proof, he gave orders that the man should be punished. The natives looked on with fixed attention while the man was being stripped and tied up to the rigging, waiting in silent suspense for the event; but as soon as the first stroke was given they interfered with great agitation, earnestly entreating that he might be forgiven. Cook, however, did not think it advisable to agree to this. He would not consent, and, when they found that their entreaties were of no avail, they gave vent to their pity in tears.

CHAPTER VII.

Shows what Vanity will induce Men and Women to do.

It fills one with wonder to think of the strange and absurd things that men, in all ages and in all parts of the world, have done to themselves in order to improve their personal appearance. The flat-head Indian of North America squeezes his forehead out of shape; the Eastern beauty blackens her teeth and nails; the Chinaman shaves the hair off his head, leaving a tuft on the top; the Englishman shaves the hair off his face, leaving a tuft on each cheek, — and all of these deluded mortals run thus deliberately in the face of nature, under the impression that by so doing they are improving their personal appearance!

Not to be behindhand, the South-Sea islanders tattoo themselves. In other words, they prick a multitude of little holes in their skins, and rub into these some colouring matter, which, when thoroughly fixed, cannot again be washed out. The ornamental devices with which they thus, more or less, cover their persons are sometimes very cleverly and tastefully done, and they would be really admirable if depicted on a piece of wood or a sheet of paper; but when applied to the human body they are altogether ridiculous.

The operation of tattooing is a very painful one; so much so, that a great deal of it cannot be done at one time, and it is said that persons sometimes die during the process. The inhabitants of nearly all the islands practise it. Usually it is commenced at the age of eight or ten, and continued at intervals till the individual is between twenty and thirty years of age.

So important and difficult is the art of tattooing, that men devote themselves to it professionally, and these professors are well paid for their work. Here is an account of the operation.

The professor, having his victim on the ground before him, takes up his instrument of torture. This consists of a small piece of stick with sharp bones of birds or fishes attached to it. Having previously sketched with a piece of charcoal the pattern intended to be tattooed, he dips the points of the sharp bones into a colouring matter (which is a beautiful jet black, procured from the kernel of the candle-nut), applies it to the surface of the skin, and strikes it smartly with a piece of stick held in his right hand. The skin is punctured in this way, and the dye injected. With the calmness of an operator, and the gravity of an artist, the professor proceeds as long as his patient can endure the pain. Then he ceases, and when the part is sufficiently recovered, the operation is continued until the device or pattern is finished.

These patterns vary among different islanders. They consist of circular and curving lines, and representations of palm-trees, animals, etc., on the face and body; and to such an extent is tattooing carried, that the whole body is sometimes covered so as nearly to conceal the original colour of the skin.

Mr. Ellis, who wrote long after the gallant Cook was in his grave, tells us in his most interesting work on the South-Sea Islands, (Ellis's *Polynesian Researches*), that the inhabitants of Tahiti were more simple in their tattooing, and displayed greater taste and elegance than some of the other islanders. "Though some of the figures are arbitrary, such as stars, circles, lozenges, etc., the patterns are usually taken from nature, and are often some of the most graceful. A cocoa-nut tree is a favourite object; and I have often admired the taste displayed in the marking of a chief's leg, on which I have seen a cocoa-nut tree correctly and distinctly drawn; its roots spreading at the heel, its elastic stalk pencilled as it were along the tendon, and its waving plume gracefully spread out on the broad part of the calf. Sometimes a couple of stems would be twined up from the heel and divide on the calf, each bearing a plume of leaves.

"The ornaments round the ankle and upon the instep, make them often appear as if they wore the elegant Eastern sandal. The sides of the legs are sometimes tattooed from the ankle upward, which gives the appearance of wearing pantaloons with ornamental seams. From the lower part of the back, a number of straight, waved, or zigzag lines rise in the direction of the spine, and branch off regularly towards the shoulder. But, of the upper part of the body, the chest is the most tattooed. Every variety of figure is to be seen here, — cocoa-nut and bread-fruit trees, with convolvulus wreaths hanging round them, boys gathering fruit, men engaged in battle, in the manual exercise, triumphing over a fallen foe; or, as I have frequently seen it, they are represented as carrying a human sacrifice to the temple. Every kind of animal — goats, dogs, fowls, and fish — may at times be seen on this part of the body; muskets, swords, pistols, clubs, spears, and other weapons of war are also stamped upon their arms and chest."

These figures are not all crowded upon the same person, but each man makes a selection according to his fancy. The women also tattoo their persons, but not to such an extent as the men, and their designs and figures are usually more tasteful.

Cook says that Mr. Banks saw this operation performed on the back of a girl about thirteen years old. The instrument used upon this occasion had thirty teeth; about a hundred strokes were given in the minute, and each stroke drew a little blood. The girl bore it bravely for about a quarter of an hour; but at the end of that time the pain of so many hundred punctures became unbearable. She first complained in murmurs, then wept, and at last burst into loud lamentations, earnestly beseeching the operator to stop. He, however, firmly refused, and when she began to struggle, she was held down by two women, who sometimes soothed and sometimes scolded her, and, now and then, when she became very unruly, gave her a smart blow. Mr. Banks stayed in a neighbouring house an hour, and the operation was not over when he went away, yet it was performed only on one side of the back; the other had been tattooed some time before, and the loins had still to be done.

Tahiti is now one of the civilised islands of the South Seas. At the time of Cook's visit the natives were absolutely savages. They lived in a state of partial nakedness, and their manners and customs were of the grossest description. Their religion and superstitions were degrading in the extreme, and, until Christianity obtained a hold upon them, they delighted in war, and practised horrible cruelties on their enemies.

Yet, even in their low condition, there were good points about those islanders. Cook says that they were as large as the largest-sized Europeans. The men were tall, strong, well-limbed, and finely shaped. The tallest he saw, on a neighbouring island, was a man who measured six feet three inches and a half. The women of the superior rank were above our middle stature, but those of the inferior class rather below it. Their complexion was a kind of clear olive or *brunette*, and the skin of the women was smooth and soft. They had no colour in their cheeks, but their faces were comely; the cheekbones were not high, neither were the eyes hollow. Their eyes were sparkling and full of expression, and their teeth good, but their noses being flat did not correspond with his ideas of beauty. Their hair was black and coarse. The men had beards, which they wore in many fashions, always, however, plucking out great part of them, and keeping the rest perfectly clean and neat.

In most countries it is the custom of the men to wear short and the women long hair. Here, however, Cook found this custom reversed. The women cut it short round the ears, and the men — except the fishermen, who were almost continually in the water — suffered it to flow in large waves over their shoulders, or tied it up in a bunch on the top of their heads. They were in the habit of anointing it with cocoa-nut oil, which had the effect of rendering their heads very filthy; but in other respects the natives of Tahiti were remarkable for cleanliness.

Their clothing consisted of native-made cloth or matting, and was very scanty, but in many cases was tastefully put on and intermingled with flowers. Some of the men wore a feather in their hair; others wore a wig made of the hair of men and dogs. Both sexes wore ear-rings made of pieces of stones, shells, or berries, which were speedily exchanged, however, for the beads given them by the sailors, for, like all other savages, they delighted in gay ornaments.

The houses of these people were very simple. They consisted of nothing more than a thatched roof mounted upon pillars. They had no walls whatever, and were open to every wind of heaven, but in so warm a climate this was not considered a disadvantage. There were no rooms or partitions of any kind in them, and they were usually large. Some belonged to families, others were the public property of a district, and these last were sometimes two hundred feet long by thirty broad.

All the houses were built in the woods that lay between the sea and the mountains. No more ground was cleared for each house than was just sufficient to prevent the droppings of the branches from falling on the roof; so that the inhabitant could step at once from his cottage into the shade of the forest, which was the most delightful and romantic that could be imagined. It consisted of groves of bread-fruit and cocoa-nut trees without underwood, and paths led in all directions through it from one house to another. Only those travellers who have experienced the intense overpowering heat of tropical countries can form a just conception of the enjoyableness of a ramble through the shady groves of Tahiti.

The food eaten by the natives was chiefly vegetable. They had tame hogs, dogs, and poultry, but these were not plentiful, and the visit of Cook's ship soon diminished the numbers of animals very considerably. When a chief killed a hog it was divided almost equally amongst his dependants, and as these were numerous, the share of each individual at a feast was not large. Dogs and fowls fell to the lot of the lower classes. Cook says that he could not commend the flavour of their fowls, but he and his crew unanimously agreed that a South-Sea dog was little inferior to English lamb! He conjectured that their excellence was owing to the fact that they were fed exclusively upon vegetables.

Like everything else in Tahiti, the art of cooking was somewhat peculiar. The preparation of a dog for dinner is thus described:

"The dog, which was very fat, we consigned over to Tupia, who undertook to perform the double office of butcher and cook. He killed him by holding his hands close over his mouth and nose, an operation which continued above a quarter of an hour. While this was going on, a hole was made in the ground about a foot deep, in which a fire was kindled, and some small stones were placed in layers alternately with the wood to get heated. The dog was then singed by holding him over the fire, and by scraping him with a shell the hair came off as clean as if he had been scalded in hot water. He was then cut up with the same instrument, and his entrails being taken out, were sent to the sea, where, being carefully washed, they were put into cocoanut shells with what blood came from the body.

"When the hole was sufficiently heated, the fire was re-moved, and some of the stones, — which were not so hot as to dis-colour anything that touched them, — being placed in the bottom, were covered with green leaves. The dog and the entrails were then placed upon the leaves, other leaves were placed above them, the whole was covered up with the remainder of the hot stones, and the mouth of the hole was closed with mould. In somewhat less than four hours it was again opened and the dog taken out excellently baked. Nearly all the fish and flesh eaten by the inhabitants is dressed in this way.

The sea in those regions affords the natives great variety of fish; the smaller of which they usually eat raw. They have also lobsters, crabs, and other shell-fish, all of which they are very fond of. Indeed, nothing seems to come amiss to them. They even eat what sailors call *blubbers*, though some of these are so tough that they have to allow them to become putrid before they can chew them.

Their chief vegetable, the bread-fruit, is so curious a plant that it merits particular notice. It costs them no more trouble or labour to procure it than the climbing of a tree. In regard to this tree Cook says that it does not indeed shoot up spontaneously, but if a man plants ten of them in his lifetime, which he may do in about an hour, he will sufficiently fulfil his duty to his own and to future generations. True, the bread-fruit is not always in season; but when its ready-made loaves are not to be had, the South-Sea islander has plenty of cocoa-nuts, bananas, plantains, and other fruits to supply its place.

The bread-fruit tree is large and beautiful. Its trunk, which is light-coloured and rough, grows to a height of twelve or twenty feet, and is sometimes three feet in diameter. Its leaves are broad, dark green, and a foot or eighteen inches long. The fruit, about the size of a child's head, is round, covered with a rough rind, and is at first of a light pea-green hue; subsequently it changes to brown, and when fully ripe, assumes a rich yellow colour. It hangs to the branches singly, or in clusters of two or three together. One of these magnificent trees, clothed with its dark shining leaves and loaded with many hundreds of large light green or yellowish fruit, is one of the most beautiful objects to be met with among the islands of the south.

The pulp of the bread-fruit between the rind and the core is all eatable. The core itself, which is about the size and shape of the handle of a knife, is uneatable. The bread-fruit is never eaten raw. The usual mode of dressing it is to remove the rind and the core, divide the pulp into three or four pieces, and bake it in an oven similar to the one just described. When taken out, in some-what less than an hour, the outside of the fruit is nicely browned, and the inner part so strongly resembles the crumb of wheaten bread as to have suggested the name of the tree. It is not, however, quite so pleasant to the taste, being rather insipid and slightly sweet. Nevertheless it is extremely good for food, and is much prized by the natives, to whom it may almost be said to be the staff of life.

The tree on which this excellent fruit grows, besides producing two, and, in some cases, three crops in a year, furnishes a species of gum, or resin, which oozes from the bark when cut, and hardens when exposed to the sun. It is used for pitching the seams of canoes. The bark of the young branches is employed in making several varieties of native cloth. The wood of the tree is also valuable for building houses and canoes. There are nearly fifty varieties of the bread-fruit tree, for which the natives have distinct names, and as these varieties ripen at different times, there are few months in the year in which the fruit is not to be had.

Not less valuable to the natives of these islands is the cocoa-nut tree, the stem of which is three or four feet in diameter at the root, whence it tapers gradually without branch or leaf to the top, where it terminates in a beautiful tuft or plume of long green leaves which wave gracefully in every breeze.

One of the singular peculiarities of this tree is its power of flourishing in almost any soil. It grows equally well on the mountain-side, in the rich valleys beside the streams, and on the barren sea-beach of the coral reefs, where its only soil is sand, and where its roots are watered by the waves of every rising tide. Another peculiarity is, that fruit in every stage may be seen on the same tree at one time – from the first formation, after the falling of the blossom, to the ripe nut. As the tree is slow in growth, the nuts do not probably come to perfection until twelve months after the blossoms have fallen. The successive ripening of the nuts, therefore, seems to have been purposely arranged by our beneficent Creator, with a special view to the comfort of man. Each nut is surrounded by a tough husk, or shell, nearly two inches thick, and when it has reached its full size it contains a pint, or a pint and a half, of the juice usually called cocoa-nut milk.

The kernels of the tough outer husks, above referred to, are the "cocoa-nuts" which we see exposed for sale in this country, but these nuts give no idea of the delightful fruit when plucked from the tree. They are old and dry, and the milk is comparatively rancid. In the state in which we usually see cocoa-nuts they are never used by the natives except as seed, or for the extraction of oil.

Some varieties of this tree grow to a height of sixty or seventy feet. As all the nuts are at the top the gathering of them would be an extremely difficult matter were it not for an ingenious contrivance by which the natives manage to climb the trees; for it may be easily understood that to *shin* up an exceedingly rough pole of seventy feet high, with bare legs, would try the mettle of most men — civilised as well as savage. The plan is simple. The native strips off a piece of tough bark from a branch, and therewith ties his feet together, leaving them, however, several inches apart, grasping the trunk with his arms he presses his feet against each side of the tree so that the piece of bark between them catches in the roughnesses of the stem; this gives him a purchase by which he is enabled to leap or vault up like a monkey.

The wood of the tree is excellent. The natives make pillars for their houses and their best spears from it. A species of what we may call natural cloth is found, ready-made, on its leaves, with which they make sacks, and shirts, and jackets. Plaited leaflets form coverings for their floors. Baskets are made from the leaves, matting and cordage of the fibrous husk, and oil is extracted from the nut. Besides all this, the shells of the old nuts are used as water-bottles, and, when carved and highly polished, they form elegant drinking-cups.

The perfect adaptation of the bread-fruit and cocoa-nut trees to the varied wants of the South-sea islanders tells, more eloquently than could be told in words, of the wisdom and benevolence with which the Almighty cares for His creatures, even while those creatures are living in the habitual neglect of Himself, and in the violation of all His laws.

CHAPTER VIII.

Treats of Savage Warfare and some of its Consequences.

It has been said that the natives of the innumerable islands of the South Seas are fond of war.

All travellers to those regions bear witness to this fact. When Cook went there, the natives of all of them were absolute savages. At the present time a great number of the islands have been blessed with the light of Christianity, but some of them are still lying in the state of degradation in which they were first found.

At this moment, reader, while you ponder these lines, there are men of the South Seas who wander about in a state of nudity and idleness; who practise every species of abomination, and kill, roast, and eat each other, just as they did a hundred years ago.

The eating of human beings, or, as it is called, cannibalism, is no idle tale invented by travellers. Men of the highest character for truth, who have had ample opportunity for observation, from the time of Cook to the present day, have assured us that the natives of those lovely regions are cannibals: that they not only eat the bodies of enemies slain in war, but even kill and eat their own slaves. Of this you shall hear more anon; meanwhile, let us turn aside to see how these savage warriors go forth to battle.

When it has been decided that they shall go to war, the natives of the South-Sea islands commence their preparations with human sacrifices to the god of war. After many strange, bloody, and superstitious rites, the warriors arm themselves and prepare for the fight.

Their weapons, which they use with great dexterity, are slings for throwing heavy stones, pikes headed with the bones of sting-rays, and clubs about six or seven feet long, made of a very hard and heavy wood. In some instances these are richly carved. The chief of each district leads his own subjects to the field, and reports the number of his men to the leading chief. When all are assembled they sally forth. If the fight is to take place on land, it is sometimes begun by the celebrated warriors of each army marching to the front of their respective lines, and sitting down on the ground. Several of these then step forward, and boastfully challenge each other to combat. The challenge is usually accepted at once, and after taunting each other for some time, they engage in furious battle. When one falls, a man from his side rises and steps forward to fill his place and continue the fight. If either party gives way, then the main body of the army to which it belongs rushes forward to its support. The opposing army of course springs forward to meet them, and thus the fight becomes general. The main bodies advance in ranks four deep. In the first rank are the bravest men, armed with spears; in the second rank they are armed with clubs to defend the spearmen. The third row consists of young men with slings, and the fourth is composed of women, who carry baskets of stones for the slingers, and clubs and spears for the other combatants.

There is no science displayed in their mode of fighting. The opposing armies rush upon each other with terrible fury, dealing deadly blows and thrusts with their murderous weapons. The din and clamour of the fray is increased by a class of men whose duty it is to animate the troops by voice and gesture. These may be styled the orators of battle, and are usually men of commanding stature and well-tried courage. They mingle in the thickest of the fight; hurry to and fro, cheering the men with the passionate recital of heroic deeds, and, in every possible way, rousing their courage and urging them on to deeds of valour. Pressing through the host with flashing eyes and thundering voice, they shout such abrupt sentences as the following:

"Roll onward like the billows! Break on them with the ocean's foam and roar when bursting on the reefs! Hang on them as the forked lightning plays above the foaming surf! Give out the vigilance; give out the anger — the anger of the devouring wild dog — till their line is broken; till they flow back like the receding tide!"

Amid such cries, mingled with the shouts of maddened combatants, and the yells of stricken men, the fight goes on. They use no shields. Believing that the gods direct their weapons, they make no attempt to guard, but lay about them with fury. Blows do not often require to be repeated. Skulls are cleft or battered in; and hearts are pierced with one blow or thrust, and, when noted warriors fall on either side, shouts of triumph echo along the line and strike a panic through the enemy's ranks.

The first wounded man who can be seized before being quite dead is offered in sacrifice by his foes. He is not taken to their temple for that purpose, but his head is bound round with sacred cinet brought from the temple, and he is then laid alive on a number of spears and borne on men's shoulders along the ranks, the priest of the god of war walking alongside and watching the writhings of the dying man. If a tear falls from his eye it is said he is weeping for his land. If he should clench his fist it is supposed to be a sign that his party will resist to the last.

If a great chief falls, the party to which he belongs retires a short distance, collects some of the bravest men, and then rushes with incredible fury and yells of vengeance upon the foe to "clear away the blood." The shock is terrific when the contending parties meet, and numbers usually fall on both sides.

During the battle the armies sometimes separate a little distance for a time, leaving a space between them; then the slingers of stones advance. The most expert of these slingers are renowned warriors, and when they are recognised a shout arises from the opposite ranks, "Beware! a powerful stone is such an one." At short range the stones about the size of a hen's egg are thrown straight at the enemy with such force that it is almost impossible to avoid them, so that they do much execution. But soon again the lines close and the fight is renewed hand to hand.

At length one of the lines begins to waver. Seeing this, the others are encouraged to renewed efforts; their enemies at last break and fly, and then a scene of terrible carnage follows. The vanquished rush to their canoes, or fly to the strongholds of the mountains. The victors continue the pursuit, slaughtering men and women indiscriminately. A fallen warrior perchance cries for mercy, "Spare me! may I live?" says he. If the name of his conqueror's chief or king is invoked, the request is sometimes granted; if not, the only reply is a taunt, followed by a thrust or a deadly blow. Thus the scene of murder and blood goes on until the fugitives have reached their strongholds, or until the shades of evening put an end to the pursuit.

Such were the scenes that took place in the days of Captain Cook, and such or similar scenes still occur frequently at the present time on the coral isles of the Pacific.

When their wars are conducted on the sea, the islanders embark in war-canoes, which are so large as to be able to carry from sixty to eighty and even a hundred men. Captain Cook tells us that the ingenuity of these people appears in nothing more than in their canoes. They are long and narrow. One that he measured was sixty-eight and a half feet long, five feet broad, and three feet and a half deep. The bottom was sharp, with straight sides like a wedge. Each side consisted of one entire plank sixty-three feet long, ten or twelve inches broad, and an inch and a quarter thick. The bottom part of the canoe was hollowed out, and these planks were lashed to it with strong plaiting. A grotesque ornament projected six feet beyond the head, and it had a sort of stern-post that rose to a height of about fourteen feet. Both the head and the stern-post were beautifully carved, and the canoe was propelled by means of short paddles, the men sitting with their faces in the direction in which they were going. The heads of many of the canoes were curious, in some cases it was the figure of a man with a face as ugly as can well be conceived, with a monstrous tongue thrust out of the mouth, and white shells stuck in for eyes.

In such canoes they went forth to war upon the water, and their sea-fights were not less sanguinary than those of the land. In one battle that was fought between the people of Huahine and those of Raiatea immense slaughter took place. The fleet of one side consisted of ninety war-canoes, each about a hundred feet long, and filled with men. They met near a place called Hooroto, when a most obstinate and bloody engagement ensued. Both parties lost so many men that, when piled up on the day after the battle, the dead bodies formed a heap "as high as the young cocoa-nut trees."

The captives taken in these wars are usually murdered on the spot, unless reserved for slaves to their conquerors.

One of the results of these sanguinary fights is the existence of a number of what may be called wild men in the mountains of the islands. Ellis, in his *Polynesian Researches*, tells us that he once saw one of these men who had been caught in the mountains and was at that time comparatively tame, yet his appearance was very remarkable. He was about the middle size, large boned, but not fleshy. His features and countenance were strongly marked. His complexion was dark, and his aspect agitated and wild. His beard was long, and the hair of his head upwards of a foot and a half in length. It was parted on his forehead, but was matted and dishevelled. The colour of his hair was singular. At the roots it was black, six inches from his head it was light brown, and the extremities were light yellow. He was quite naked, with the exception of a *maro* or girdle round the loins. This poor creature had been driven to the mountains in time of war, and had remained in solitude for many years. Probably extreme terror had affected his mind, for he was gloomy, and seemed to take no interest in anything going on around him. Evidently those "wild men" were poor creatures whose misfortunes had driven them mad.

One of them was captured on another occasion by a party which had gone into the mountains to collect the bark of a certain tree which is used for dyeing cloth. On their way they perceived a man lying asleep on the ground. They surrounded him with as little noise as possible, but when they approached he awoke. Leaping up, he flung his wild locks over his shoulders and gazed at them with a startled look; then he darted into the woods, where he was caught by one of the men and secured. Had he not been enfeebled from recent illness, they could neither have caught nor retained this man.

On being taken he exhibited signs of extreme terror. It was in vain that his captors assured him they meant him no harm; he continued to exclaim, "Ye are murderers, ye are murderers! do not murder me, do not murder me!" Even after he had been taken to the settlement and treated with great kindness, he could not be prevailed on to say anything more than "Do not kill me," and did not rest until he had made his escape into the woods!

CHAPTER IX.

Touches on Cannibalism.

The cruelties inflicted on the wretched prisoners taken in these wars were inconceivably horrible and disgusting. Some of our readers may, perhaps, think we might have passed over the sickening details in silence, but we feel strongly that it is better that truth should be known than that the feelings of the sensitive should be spared.

Ellis tells us that the bodies of men slain in battle were usually left to be devoured by the hogs and wild dogs. This was doubtless the case in some of the groups of islands where cannibalism was perhaps not very much practised, but in other groups — especially among those known by the name of the Feejees — the slain were more frequently devoured by men and women than by hogs or dogs. The victors used to carry off the lower jaw-bones of the most distinguished among the slain as trophies, and also the bones of the arms and legs, from which they formed tools of various kinds and fish-hooks, and the skulls they converted into drinking-cups. The dead bodies were sometimes laid in rows along the beach, and used as rollers, over which the canoes were launched.

One of their practices with the dead was ludicrously horrible. Sometimes, when a man had slain his enemy, in order to gratify his revenge he would beat the body quite flat, and then, cutting a hole through the back and stomach, would pass his head through it and actually rush into the fight wearing the body round his neck, with the head and arms hanging down in front, and the legs behind!

The bodies of celebrated warriors and chiefs were hung by a rope to a tree, after the legs and arms had been broken; cords were attached to their feet, and then they were drawn up and down for the amusement of the spectators, while other dead bodies were beaten as drums, to make a hideous music to this horrible dance.

Other brutalities were practised upon the slain, which were of such a nature that decency forbids our doing more than merely alluding to them here. In order to show that many of the savages of the South Seas were as bad, only a few years ago, as they were in former times, we give the following account of a scene which is published and vouched for in a recent work, named the *Journal of a Cruise among the Islands of the Western Pacific*, by Captain Erskine of the Royal Navy.

About twenty years ago Bonavidongo, one of the chiefs of the Feejee Islands, paid a visit to another chief named Tuithakau, for the purpose of asking his assistance in quelling a disturbance that had arisen in a neighbouring island. The latter agreed; all the warriors of the island and the surrounding district were gathered together, and an army of two thousand men finally set forth on this expedition in forty war-canoes.

Among the people was an English sailor named Jackson. He was of a roving disposition; had been kidnapped at one of the islands, from which he escaped, and afterwards wandered for two years among the South-Sea Islands — learned the language of the natives, and wrote an account of his adventures, which Captain Erskine added to his volume in the form of an appendix.

Not being able to carry provisions for so large a body of men for any length of time, the Feejeeans made a short stay at a place called Rambe, for the purpose of refreshing the people. Here they procured immense quantities of yams and crabs, with which, after eating and drinking to their hearts' content, they loaded the canoes and continued the voyage. From Rambe, as well as from other places along the route, they were joined by additional canoes and warriors, so that their numbers rapidly increased. Frequently they were obliged to sleep in the canoes instead of on shore, on which occasions they were jammed up in such a manner from want of space as to be actually lying in layers on the top of each other!

At one place where they called they could not obtain a sufficient supply of provisions for the whole party on account of its being small and containing but few inhabitants, so they made up the deficiency with dogs, cats, snakes, lizards, and the large white grubs with black heads that are found in decayed wood. The dogs and cats they knocked on the head, more for the purpose of stunning than killing, and threw them on a fire, and, after letting them lie five minutes or so on one side, turned them over on the other, then drew them from the fire and devoured them. The grubs they ate raw.

Jackson was much surprised at what he terms, "this beastly way of feeding," because in his previous experience he had found the Feejeeans to be extremely particular in all preparations of food. On inquiring the cause of the change, however, he was informed, "that they felt proud that they were able to endure such hard fare, and that it was essential to their warlike customs, as they could not expect to sleep as well in war-time as in peace, and that they must endure every inconvenience, and pay no attention whatever to comfort!"

At length they arrived at the island of Mouta, where they landed to announce their arrival to the king, and to present him with a gift of whales' teeth, which are much prized, and used on nearly all such occasions. In order to reach the town they had to proceed up a long, serpentine, narrow river, each bank of which was so thickly covered with mangrove trees that they overshadowed it completely — rendering it exceedingly dark and dismal. In the middle of the town stood the king's house, and directly opposite was the "bure," or temple. The whole town contained about one hundred and fifty houses.

Having presented the whales' teeth to his savage majesty, they related all that had happened on the voyage, detailing the minutest particulars, after which they went to the temple to do honour to the god of war; and here the story of the voyage was repeated to the priest, who replied in a long speech. This speech was listened to with the deepest attention, because it was considered prophetic. The priest finished off by encouraging all present to be obedient to the god of war, and to do their best to gratify his appetite, adding, that the success of the whole expedition depended on their obedience. He reminded them that the god was a great lover of animal food, especially of human flesh. Jackson afterwards found that the appetite of the priest was quite as peculiar and strong as that of the god in this respect, and that the king was a greater cannibal than the priest!

Next morning they re-embarked and started for Male, in the disturbed district. The inhabitants of Male lived on the top of a mountain shaped like a sugar-loaf, and having only one path leading up it. At the top this path could be easily defended by a small body of men against ten times their number, as they could roll down large stones upon their enemies while they approached. Knowing the strength of their position, the natives of this place had become the pest of the neighbourhood. They sallied forth and committed great depredations on the villages near them — carrying away the women into slavery, and killing the men for food!

On approaching the place the war-party saw that the natives, by their antics, were challenging and defying them. When they landed and could hear what they said, they made out their speech of defiance to be, "We are extremely tired of waiting for you, especially as we have been expecting this visit so long: but as you have at last made your appearance, we are quite ready to begin at once. We would remind you, at the same time, that we are well supplied with stones, and, if these fail, we have also a good store of British sand (gunpowder), and plenty of pills (musket-balls), which we will bestow upon you very generously. We see that you have got the Feejees and Tongas with you, but we hope you will not have the folly and impudence to attack us until you have collected the whole world to help you!"

To this contemptuous speech the war-party made a somewhat similar reply. After they had thus abused each other for some time, three of the people of the hill ventured half-way down the path, where they stood and dared any, or the whole, of their enemies to come up. As it was not, however, the intention of the war-party to assault the stronghold at that time, they declined the invitation, but, happening to possess several old muskets, which they had procured, no doubt, from traders, they fired a volley at the three challengers, killed them all on the spot, and, rushing up, caught the bodies as they rolled down the path.

The corpses were then fastened to a pole in a sitting posture, and placed in the canoe of the chief, who resumed his voyage, his warriors singing out, "Satiko, satiko" (Good-bye, good-bye), and telling the people of Male that they would call again upon them shortly, as their place was so conveniently situated, and take a few more bodies, just enough at a time for the priest of the god of war — in short, that they would take them in the same way as a man kills his pigs; and they were to be sure to feed themselves well, for their chief was fond of fat meat!

With this supply of food they returned to Mouta. Here the bodies, which had been carefully painted with vermilion and soot, were handed out and placed, sitting up, in front of the king's house; but before proceeding to their loathsome banquet they enacted scenes in which there was a dreadful mingling of the ludicrous and the horrible.

The whole of the people being assembled, and dead silence secured, an old man advanced to the bodies, and, laying his hand upon each, began talking to it in a low tone, asking it, "why he had been so rash in coming down the hill," and telling it, "that he was extremely sorry to see him in such a predicament; and did he not feel ashamed of himself now that he was obliged to encounter the gaze of such a crowd." By degrees the old orator worked himself into a state of excitement, till at last he shouted at the full strength of his voice, and finally finished off by kicking the bodies down, amid bursts of laughter from tho spectators, who then rushed forward, and, seizing each by a leg or an arm, dragged them over stones and dust and swamps for the general amusement of the people.

At last they pulled them up to a place at the back of the town which was used for the purpose of cutting up, cooking, and eating human flesh. In front of this dreadful place lay a heap of human bones bleached by the weather. Here the priest was seated, with his long beard hanging down on a little table before him. On this table were two skulls converted into drinking-cups, and several others were lying about the floor.

Without going further into the disgusting details, it may be sufficient to add that the three bodies were cut up by the priest and cooked in an oven heated by means of hot stones, after which they were devoured as a great treat, and with infinite relish, by the king and his chief men.

It was long before people in the civilised world would give credit to stories such as that just related; and even now there may be some who doubt the truth of them. But the number and the characters of the travellers who have visited these islands since the days of Cook, and who have brought home similar reports, put the matter beyond question. Men ought neither to doubt these shocking details because they seem incredible, nor turn away from them because they are disgusting. Like the surgeon who calmly and steadily examines the most hideous of wounds or sores that can affect the human body, so ought the Christian and the philanthropist to know and consider in detail the horrible deeds that are done by our fellow-men in the Cannibal Islands. It is good for us to be made acquainted with the truth in order that we may be filled with strong pity for the degraded savages, and in order, also, that our hearts and hands may be opened towards those noble missionaries who venture themselves into the midst of such awful scenes for the sake of souls, and in the name of Jesus Christ.

CHAPTER X.

Visit to New Zealand.

Captain Cook left Tahiti after a stay of three months. During the greater part of this period the sailors and natives had lived together in the most cordial friendship, and in the perpetual interchange of kindly acts. It must be borne in mind that, though the unchristianised natives of the South-Sea Islands are all degraded, cruel, and savage, all are not equally so. Those inhabiting the Feejee group are generally reported to be the worst in all respects. Those who inhabited Tahiti, on the other hand, were, at the time of Cook's visit, said to be comparatively amiable.

At all events, the departure of the *Endeavour* called forth a strong display of tender feeling on the part of the natives of that island. In writing of this Cook says —

"On the next morning, Thursday, the 13th July, the ship was very early crowded with our friends, and surrounded by multitudes of canoes, which were filled with natives of an inferior class. Between eleven and twelve we weighed anchor, and as soon as the ship was under sail the Indians on board took their leave, and wept with a decent and silent sorrow, in which there was something very striking and tender. The people in the canoes, on the contrary, seemed to vie with each other in the loudness of their lamentations, which we considered rather as an affectation than grief. Tupia (a chief who had made up his mind to sail with us) sustained himself in this scene with a firmness and resolution truly admirable. He wept, indeed, but the effort that he made to conceal his tears concurred with them to do him honour. He sent his last present, a shirt, to a friend on shore, and then went to the mast-head, where he continued waving to the canoes as long as they were in sight."

Thus ended the visit of the great navigator to Tahiti, an island which afterwards became the scene of one of the most romantic incidents that was ever recorded in the annals of maritime adventure, namely, the mutiny of the men in H.M.S. *Bounty*, and the consequent colonisation of Pitcairn Island. Tahiti is now civilised, and under the protective government of the French. The produce of the island is bread-fruit, cocoa-nuts, bananas of thirteen sorts, plantains, a fruit not unlike an apple, which, when ripe, is very pleasant, sweet potatoes, yams, sugar-cane, which the natives eat raw, besides many other kinds of fruits, roots, and vegetables, all of which grew wild when Cook was there, or with so little culture that the islanders are almost altogether exempted from labour.

Setting sail from Tahiti, the *Endeavour* visited several other isles, and at length arrived at the celebrated island of New Zealand. This is one of the largest in the South Seas, and is now the site of several thriving British settlements. Flourishing cities have been built on its rich soil; large portions of it have been brought under cultivation; gold-mines have been discovered; churches and schools have been erected, and many of the natives have become partially civilised.

Very different indeed was the state of things when Captain Cook first drew near to its shores in the year 1769.

He cast anchor on the 8th of October in a bay near the mouth of a small river about half a league from shore. The sides of the bay were white cliffs of great height, and inland the hills rose one behind another, towering upwards until they terminated in a chain of mountains in the far distance. Some natives had been seen on the beach, so, when the ship was secured, Cook took two of his boats, and, accompanied by Mr. Banks and Dr. Solander, with a party of men, went on shore. They landed on the east side of the river, but finding it too deep to cross, and seeing some natives on the other side, they took one of the boats – the yawl – and went over, leaving the other boat – the pinnace – behind them.

When the navigators drew near to the place where the natives were assembled, the latter ran away. The sailors then landed, and, leaving four boys in charge of the boat, walked up to some huts which were two or three hundred yards from the beach. But they had not gone far from the water-side when four men, armed with long lances, rushed out of the woods, and ran to attack the boat. They would certainly have succeeded in over-powering the four boys and making off with the boat, had they not fortunately been seen by the people left in the pinnace, who called out to warn the boys of their danger, telling them to push off and drop down stream. The boys obeyed instantly. Being closely pursued by the savages, one of them fired a musket over their heads.

At this they stopped in surprise and looked round them, but in a few minutes renewed the pursuit, brandishing their lances in a threatening manner, as if about to cast them into the boat, which they could easily have done. The boys then fired a second shot over their heads, but of this they took no notice, and one of them lifted his spear with the intention of darting it; another musket was therefore fired, which shot the savage dead. When he fell the other three stood motionless for some time, as if petrified with astonishment. As soon as they recovered they went back to the woods, dragging the dead body, but they soon dropped it and fled when they saw Cook and his companions running to the rescue.

The dead body was examined, and found to be that of a man of middle size, with brown complexion and a tattooed face. He was covered with a kind of native cloth, and wore his hair tied up in a knot on the top of his head. Cook immediately returned to the ship, from the deck of which he could hear the voices of the natives on shore talking with great earnestness and in a very loud tone.

Being anxious to enter into friendly intercourse with these people, Cook renewed the attempt next morning. He ordered three boats to be manned with seamen and marines, and proceeded towards the shore, accompanied by Mr. Banks and Dr. Solander, also by Tupia, the Tahitan, to act as interpreter. About fifty natives came to the beach and sat down to await their landing. In order to prevent them taking fright, Cook landed first and advanced, accompanied only by the two gentlemen above named and Tupia. But they had not proceeded many paces before the savages started up, and every man produced either a long pike or a small weapon of green talc extremely well polished, about a foot long, and thick enough to weigh four or five pounds. Tupia endeavoured to appease them, but this could not be managed until a musket was fired wide of them. The ball struck the water, and on observing its effect they ceased their menaces.

Meanwhile the marines were landed and marched to a commanding position, where they were drawn up, while Captain Cook again advanced. When they came near enough, Tupia explained that they wanted provisions and water, for which they would give iron in exchange. He then asked them to lay down their arms, but they would not consent to do so. The river still lay between the two parties, and Cook invited the natives to come over and trade. They were unwilling at first, but in a short time one, bolder than the rest, stripped himself and swam over without his arms. He was immediately followed by two or three more, and soon after by most of the others. These last, however, brought their arms with them.

Presents of iron and beads were now made to the savages, but they seemed to care little for these things, and in a few minutes they attempted to snatch the arms out of the sailors' hands. In this they failed, and Cook ordered Tupia to tell them that if they tried to do that again, he would be compelled to kill them. In a few minutes Mr. Green, one of the gentlemen, happened to turn about; immediately one of them snatched away his sword and ran to a little distance, waving it round his head with a shout of triumph. Seeing this, the rest became extremely insolent, and more savages came to join them from the other side of the river. It therefore became necessary to check them, and Mr. Banks fired with small-shot at the man who had taken the sword. The shot had only the effect of stopping his shouts and causing him to retire a little farther off, still flourishing the sword, however. Seeing this, Mr. Monkhouse fired with ball, and the man dropt instantly. Upon this the main body of the natives, who had retired to a rock in the middle of the river, began to return. Two that were near the man who had been killed ran to the body, and one seized his weapon of green talc, while the other tried to secure the sword, but Mr. Monkhouse ran up in time to prevent this. Three muskets loaded with small-shot were then fired at the party, which wounded several, and caused them to retire to the opposite side of the river, after which Cook returned to the ship.

This was a matter of great disappointment to the voyagers, because they were much in want of fresh water. Cook now resolved to seize some of the natives if possible, and prove to them, by kind treatment, that they had nothing to fear. Soon after he had an opportunity of trying this plan. Two canoes were seen coming in from sea; one under sail, the other worked by paddles. Taking three boats full of men he gave chase to them; but the people in the nearest canoe perceived them, and turning aside made with all possible haste for a point of land and escaped. The other canoe was intercepted, and Tupia called to them to come alongside and they would receive no harm; but they took down the sail, took to their paddles, and made off so quickly that the boats could not overtake them. Cook then ordered a musket-ball to be fired over them. On hearing the shots they stopped paddling and began to strip, intending, no doubt, to leap into the sea. But they quickly changed their minds and resolved not to fly but to fight. When the boats came up they began the attack with their paddles and with stones so vigorously, that the voyagers were obliged to fire at them in self-defence. Unhappily four were killed, and the three who remained leaped into the sea.

These were soon captured, and were found to be mere boys — the eldest about nineteen, and the youngest about eleven. Cook deeply regretted this unfortunate affair, and blamed himself for it, but remarked, in justification of himself, that, "when the command has once been given to fire, no man can restrain its excess or prescribe its effect."

As soon as the poor wretches were taken out of the water into the boat they squatted down, expecting, no doubt, to be instantly put to death. But when they found that instead of being killed they were treated with kindness, they became exceedingly joyful. On reaching the ship they were offered some bread, which they devoured with a voracious appetite. They asked and answered a great many questions, and when the people sat down to dinner expressed a desire to touch and taste everything they saw. The food that pleased them most was salt pork. At night they made a hearty supper, and after they had each drunk above a quart of water, they lay down to sleep on a locker well pleased with their treatment.

During the night, however, their true condition as prisoners seemed to be impressed on them. Possibly they thought of their slain friends, for they began to moan dismally, and it was all Tupia could do to comfort them. Next morning they devoured an enormous breakfast, after which they were dressed, and adorned with bracelet, anklets, necklaces, etc., and sent on shore in the hope that they might carry a good report of the strangers to their friends. Nothing came of this, however, at the time. The natives still remained unfriendly, and Cook finally weighed anchor and set sail in search of a part of the coast where the people, it was hoped, would be more hospitable.

Soon after this a number of canoes came off to the ship, and the natives, to the number of fifty, came on board without fear, saying that they had heard such an account of the kindness of the sailors from the three boys, that they had come to trade with them. And they did trade with them, to such an extent that they parted with everything they had, even stripping off their clothes, and offering them in exchange for trinkets of little value!

About an hour before sunset, the canoes put off from the ship to return to shore, and then it was discovered that three natives had been left behind. Tupia hailed the canoes and told them of this, but they would not return; and what seemed more surprising, the three savages did not seem to care but remained on board eating and drinking, and entertaining the ship's company with dancing and singing of a very remarkable kind, after which they had their suppers and went quietly to bed. But they were dreadfully horrified on awaking next morning to find that the ship was sailing swiftly away with them; and they remained in a state of consternation until a canoe happened to put off from shore, and after much persuasion came alongside and took them away. The men in the canoe were very timid about coming on deck, and they could not be got to do so until the three savages assured them that the white people "did not eat men!"

Cook then continued his voyage of discovery round New Zealand, making careful notes of the coast, and naming the various headlands as he went. As the island is fully as large as Great Britain, it took him some time to accomplish the survey. He had many adventures, and saw many strange things by the way, besides running considerable danger from the natives, who showed themselves extremely hostile.

On one occasion, while they were entangled among some shoals, the hurry on board in working the ship led the savages to suppose the voyagers were alarmed, so taking advantage of this, four large canoes full of armed men put off and came towards them with the intention, apparently, of making an attack. A musket was fired over them, but as it did no harm they continued to come on. A four-pounder, loaded with grape, was then fired a little to one side of them. This caused them all to start up with a shout of surprise, after which they returned quietly to the shore.

On all occasions Captain Cook exerted himself to the utmost to prevent bloodshed; but the natives were everywhere so warlike and treacherous, that this could not always be avoided.

One day several canoes full of armed men came alongside, and were induced to trade – exchanging native cloth and arms for the usual trinkets. Tupia, the interpreter, had a little son with him named Tayeto. This little fellow was employed to stand outside the bulwarks of the ship to hand down the things from the ship to the savages in the canoes. One of these rascals, watching his opportunity, suddenly seized the lad and dragged him down into the canoe. Two of them held him down in the fore part of it, and the others with great activity paddled off – the rest of the canoes following as fast as they could.

Upon this the marines were ordered to fire. The shot was directed to that part of the canoe which was farthest from the boy. One man dropped, upon which the others quitted their hold of the boy, who sprang nimbly into the water and swam towards the ship. A large canoe turned to recapture him, but some muskets and a great gun being fired at it, the rowers desisted from farther pursuit. The ship was immediately brought to, a boat was lowered, and poor Tayeto was picked up, very much terrified, but unhurt, and none the worse for his adventure.

After this the discoverers had the most convincing proof that the inhabitants of New Zealand were cannibals. One day Mr. Banks, Dr. Solander, Tupia, and others, went ashore and visited a party of natives who appeared to have just concluded a repast. The body of a dog was found buried in their oven, and many provision-baskets stood around. In one of these they observed two bones, pretty cleanly picked, which did not seem to be the bones of a dog. On nearer inspection they were found to be those of a human being. That the flesh belonging to them had been eaten was evident, for that which remained had manifestly been dressed by fire, and in the gristles at the ends were the marks of the teeth which had gnawed them. To put an end to doubt, Tupia asked what bones they were, and the natives answered without the least hesitation that they were the bones of a man, and they had eaten the flesh off them. Upon one of the visitors pretending not to believe this, and saying that they were the bones of a dog, a native seized his own forearm with his teeth and made a show of eating it with great relish. He also took one of the bones which Mr. Banks held in his hand and bit and gnawed it, drawing it through his lips, and showing by signs that it afforded a delicious repast!

As if to relieve, somewhat, the feelings of disgust with which they were oppressed by such sights, the voyagers were regaled with the most delicious music on the following morning. About two o'clock they were awakened by the sweet singing of birds, the number of which was incredible, and their energy so great that they appeared to strain their throats in emulation of each other. This wild melody was infinitely superior to anything they had ever heard of the same kind; it seemed to be like small bells most exquisitely tuned; – perhaps the distance of the ship from shore, and the water between, may have lent additional charms to the sound.

Ere long the birds ceased to sing, and the disagreeable subject of the previous day was recalled by the appearance of a small canoe, in which was an old man, who, on coming on deck, at once revived the conversation about eating human flesh.

"But," said Tupia, after some minutes' talk, "I did not see any heads of your enemies; what do you do with them? do you not eat them too?"

"No," replied the old man, "we only eat the brains, and the next time I come I will bring off some of them to convince you that what I have told you is true."

That same day some of the sailors found on shore near an oven three human hip-bones, which they brought on board, and Mr. Monkhouse, the surgeon, discovered and took on board the hair of a man's head.

Here also they saw practised a remarkably simple and ingenious method of catching fish, which we think might be tried with advantage on our own coasts. Happening to observe a man in his canoe fishing, they rowed alongside and asked him to draw up his line, which he readily did. At the end of it they found a net of a circular form, extended by two hoops about seven or eight feet in diameter. The top was open, and sea-ears were fastened to the bottom as bait. This he let down so as to lie upon the ground until he thought fish enough had assembled over it. Then he drew it up by an extremely gentle and even motion, so that the fish rose with it, scarcely sensible (it is supposed) that they were being lifted, until near the surface of the water, when they were brought out in the net by a sudden pull!

The ingenuity of the New Zealanders appeared in nothing more than in their canoes, of which the following description is in Cook's own words:

"They are long and narrow, and in shape very much resemble a New England whale-boat; the larger sort seem to be built chiefly for war, and will carry from forty to eighty or a hundred armed men. We measured one which lay ashore at Tolago. She was sixty-eight feet and a half long, five feet broad, and three feet and a half deep. The bottom was sharp, with straight sides like a wedge, and consisted of three lengths hollowed out to about two inches, or an inch and a half thick, and well fastened together with strong plaiting. Each side consisted of one entire plank sixty-three feet long, ten or twelve inches broad, and about an inch and a quarter thick, and these were fitted and lashed to the bottom part with great dexterity and strength. A considerable number of thwarts were laid from gunwale to gunwale, to which they were securely lashed on each side, as a strengthening to the boat. The ornament at the head projected five or six feet beyond the body, and was about four feet and a half high. The ornament at the stern was fixed upon that end as the stern-post of a ship is fixed upon its keel, and was about fourteen feet high, two feet broad, and an inch and a half thick. They both consisted of boards of carved work, of which the design was much better than the execution."

The smaller canoes, which were of one piece hollowed out by fire, usually had "outriggers," — boards projecting from, and parallel to, the canoes — to prevent their overturning, and occasionally two canoes were joined together for the same purpose, as, if unsupported, they were extremely liable to upset.

The tools with which these canoes and their other implements and utensils were made consisted of axes and adzes made of a hard black stone, or of a green talc, which latter stone is not only hard but tough. They had chisels made of small fragments of jasper, and of human bones. These also served the purpose of augers for boring holes. Fish-hooks were of bone or shell; these, however, were not well made, but in the fabrication of most of their implements, canoes, war-clubs, baskets, etc., they displayed a considerable degree of taste, neatness of hand, and ingenuity.

Our space forbids us following Captain Cook very closely in his many voyages throughout the great archipelago of the South Seas. In this volume we have touched but lightly here and there on the immense variety of subjects which came under his observation. Those who wish for fuller information will find it in the work entitled *The Voyages of Captain Cook round the World*, which contains his own most interesting journals.

Passing over the years which intervene between the period of which we have been writing and the last voyage he ever made to the islands of the South Seas, we leap at once, in the next chapter, to the sad closing scenes of the great navigator's career.

CHAPTER XI.

The Last Voyage and Sad End of the Great Discoverer.

In the spring of 1776 Captain Cook set sail on his last voyage, in command of the *Resolution*, accompanied by the *Discovery* under Captain Clerke, an able officer, who had been Cook's second lieutenant on board the *Resolution* in his second voyage round the world.

The expedition was well supplied with everything that might conduce to its success, or to the comfort of those engaged in it, and many useful articles were put on board to be given to the South-Sea islanders, with a view to improve their condition — among other things, some live-stock, which, it was hoped, would multiply on the islands — such as a bull, and two cows with their calves, and some sheep; besides a quantity of such European garden seeds as were likely to thrive in those regions.

It says much for the perseverance and energy of Captain Cook that, although his education had been so defective that he only began to study Euclid and Astronomy at the age of thirty-one, he was nevertheless competent to conduct, without the aid of a scientific man, the astronomical department of this voyage.

The vessels touched at the Cape of Good Hope in passing, and sailed thence on their voyage of discovery, which extended over three years, during which period they visited Van Diemen's land, on the south of Australia, New Zealand, the Society Islands, Sandwich Islands, and other groups of the Pacific; also the western and northern coasts of North America, and saw new and beautiful regions, as well as strange and wonderful – in some cases terrible – sights, the mere enumeration of which, without going into detail, would fill many pages. We hasten, therefore, to that point in the narrative which describes the visit of the expedition to the island of Owhyhee, where its heroic commander terminated his brilliant career.

On January 1779 the *Resolution* and the *Discovery* put into a large bay named Karakakooa on the west of the island, for the purpose of refitting the ships and laying in an additional supply of water and provisions. They moored on the north side of the bay, about quarter of a mile from the shore. Here they were well received by the inhabitants, who at first were extremely hospitable. Captain King, in his journal of the transactions at this place, writes:

"As soon as the inhabitants perceived our intention of anchoring in the bay, they came off in astonishing numbers, and expressed their joy by singing and shouting, and exhibiting a variety of wild and extravagant gestures. The sides, the decks, and rigging of both ships were soon completely covered with them, and a multitude of women and boys, who had not been able to get canoes, came swimming round us in shoals; many of them not finding room on board, remained the whole day playing in the water!"

Afterwards Captain Cook went ashore and was received with many extraordinary ceremonies, which bore a strong resemblance to religious worship, but in regard to this he and his companions could only form conjectures, and were very glad to find that their entertainers were so friendly. Next morning Captain King went ashore with a guard of eight marines to erect an observatory in such a situation as might best enable him to superintend and protect the waterers and other working parties that were to be on shore. The spot chosen was immediately marked off with wands by the friendly native priests, who thus consecrated the ground, or placed it under "taboo" — a sort of religious interdiction, which effectually protected it from the intrusion of the natives — for none ever ventured, during their stay, to enter within the *tabooed* space without permission.

Very different was it on board the ships. These, not being tabooed, were overwhelmed with visitors, particularly women, who flocked on board in such numbers that the men were obliged to clear the decks almost every hour in order to have room to attend to their duties — on which occasions two or three hundred women were frequently made to jump into the water at once, where they continued swimming and playing about until they could again obtain admittance!

While, however, the priests of the island were very attentive to their visitors — sending them gifts of pigs and vegetables with extreme liberality, and expecting nothing in return, the warrior chiefs were not so disinterested. They expected and received many gifts, and they were so much addicted to theft that a constant watch had to be kept upon them, while examples had occasionally to be made of those who were caught in the act. Soon after their arrival the ships were visited in state by the King of the island, whose name was Terreeoboo. Some of his chiefs accompanied him, and all of them were dressed in rich feathered cloaks and helmets, and armed with long spears and daggers. Along with them they brought their idols, which were gigantic busts made of wicker-work, curiously covered with small feathers. Their eyes were made of large pearl oysters, with a black nut fixed in the centre of each; double rows of dogs' teeth ornamented their mouths, and their features were strangely distorted. The King and his friends were hospitably received. Presents were made, and expressions of good-will and friendship interchanged.

Thus everything went on prosperously. The refitting and

provisioning were completed; games and ceremonies were witnessed; and finally the ships left the island with the good wishes of a people who had treated their visitors with singular kindness and hospitality during the whole period of their sojourn.

Unfortunately, soon afterwards, the *Resolution* was so much damaged in a gale, that it was found necessary to return to Karakakooa Bay for repairs. To the surprise of the voyagers their reception on this occasion was very different from what it had been at first. There was no shouting, no bustle, no coming off in shoals – only here and there a canoe was seen stealing along the solitary shore. On inquiry, they were told that King Terreeoboo was absent, and had laid the bay under taboo! This looked very suspicious. However, as there was no help for it, they landed their men with the foremast of one of the ships, which required repair, and for two or three days pushed forward their work busily, expecting that when the king returned and removed the interdict, the natives would flock round them with the same good feeling as before.

Things went on in their usual quiet way till the afternoon of the 13th of February. On the evening of that day the watering-party was interfered with by natives who had armed themselves with stones, and were becoming very insolent. On the appearance, however, of Captain King with one of the marines, they threw away the stones, and some of the chiefs drove the mob away. Captain Cook, on hearing of this, ordered the sentinels to load with ball, and to fire if the interference should be repeated. Soon after that the party on shore were alarmed by a fire of musketry from the *Discovery*. It was directed at a small canoe which was paddling to the shore in great haste, pursued by one of the ship's boats. The canoe reached the shore first, and the natives, who had been stealing, made their escape. Captain Cook and Captain King pursued them into the woods for about three miles, but failed to overtake them.

During Cook's absence a serious difference occurred on the shore. One of the officers conceived it to be his duty to seize one of the native canoes. This chanced to belong to a great man named Pareea, who soon afterwards claimed his property. The officer refused to give it up, and a scuffle ensued, in which Pareea was knocked on the head with an oar. The natives immediately attacked the sailors with a shower of stones, which compelled them to retreat precipitately into the sea and swim off to a rock at some distance from the shore, leaving the pinnace in the hands of the natives, who at once ransacked it. They would probably have demolished it entirely had not Pareea, who soon recovered from his blow, come forward, and, with an admirable spirit of forgiveness, rescued it from their hands, returned it to the sailors, and afterwards rubbed noses with the officer who caused all the mischief, in token of his reconciliation!

During that night the cutter of the *Discovery* was stolen, and next morning Captain Cook, landing with nine marines, went up to the village. It had been his usual practice, whenever any-thing of importance was lost at any of the islands in that ocean, to get the king or some of the chief men on board, and keep them as hostages until the missing article should be restored. This method, which had been always attended with success, he meant to pursue on the present occasion. Meanwhile, the boats of both ships were ordered out, and well manned and armed.

Captain Cook then marched into the village, where he was received with the usual marks of respect — the people prostrating themselves before him, and bringing him their accustomed offer-ings of small hogs.

We cannot help remarking here that Cook was to be blamed for permitting the natives to treat him with a degree of ceremo-nious solemnity which was obviously meant as an act of worship.

The only thing that can be said in his defence, we think, is, that in a region where many remarkable, and to him incomprehensible, customs prevailed, he could not certainly assure himself that the people were not paying to him the ordinary homage which they were accustomed to pay to every great chief who visited their island.

He found the old king just awakening from sleep, and, after a short conversation about the loss of the cutter, the captain invited him to return in the boat and spend the day on board the *Resolution*. The king readily consented, but while on his way to the beach one of his wives, who evidently suspected treachery, besought him with many tears not to go on board. At the same time, two of his chiefs laid hold of him, and, insisting that he should go no farther, forced him to sit down. The natives had by this time collected in prodigious numbers, and the Englishmen were so surrounded that it would have been impossible for them to use their arms if any occasion had required it. Captain Cook, therefore, was obliged to give up his efforts to induce the old king to go on board.

As yet the captain had not expected or feared any attempt at personal violence, and it is probable that he would have succeeded in coming off scatheless on this occasion, as he had done many a time before, had not an unfortunate incident occurred, which gave a fatal turn to the affair. The boats of the ship, which had been stationed across the bay, fired at some canoes that were attempting to escape, and unfortunately killed a chief of the first rank. The news of his death reached the village just as Captain Cook was leaving the king, and the excitement occasioned was very great. One evidence that the natives meant to be revenged was that all the women and children were immediately sent off, and they made their intention still more apparent by putting on their war-mats, and arming themselves with spears and stones.

Just before this, however, the nine marines had been ordered to extricate themselves from the crowd and line the rocks along the shore.

One of the natives having a stone in one hand, and a long iron spike in the other, came up to the captain in a defiant manner, flourishing his weapon, and threatening to throw the stone. Cook told him to desist, but he persisted in his threatening actions, and at length provoked the captain to fire a charge of small-shot into him, having on his war-mat, however, it had no other effect than to stir up his wrath. Several stones were now thrown at the marines, and a native attempted to stab one of the party with his spear; in this, however, he failed, and was knocked down with the butt-end of a musket.

Captain Cook now felt that the safety of the party depended on prompt, decisive action, for the more he exercised forbearance the more did the savages threaten. He therefore fired his second barrel, which was loaded with ball, and killed one of the foremost.

A general attack with stones immediately followed. This was met by a discharge of muskets from the marines and the people in the boats. Contrary to expectation, the natives stood the fire with great firmness. From the accounts given of the transaction, it would appear that all the marines had discharged their muskets — none having reserved fire. This was a fatal mistake, because, before they had time to reload the natives rushed upon them in overwhelming numbers, and with fearful yells. Then followed a scene of indescribable horror and confusion.

Captain King, Cook's intimate friend, says, in regard to this closing scene, that four of the marines were cut off among the rocks in their retreat, and fell a sacrifice to the fury of the enemy; three more were dangerously wounded. The lieutenant, who had received a stab between the shoulders with a *pahooa*, having fortunately reserved his fire, shot the man who had wounded him just as he was going to repeat the blow. The unfortunate Captain Cook, when last seen distinctly, was standing at the water's edge, calling out to the men in the boats to cease firing and to pull in. If it be true, as some of those who were present have imagined, that the marines and boatmen had fired without his orders, and that he was desirous of preventing further bloodshed, it is not improbable that his humanity, on this occasion, proved fatal to him; for it was remarked that while he faced the natives none of them had offered him any violence, but that having turned about to give his order to the boats, he was stabbed in the back, and fell with his face into the water.

On seeing him fall the savages gave a great shout, rushed upon him, and dragged him on shore. They then surrounded him, and, snatching the daggers out of each other's hands, showed a savage eagerness to have a share in his destruction.

"Thus," continues King, "fell our great and excellent commander! After a life of so much distinguished and successful enterprise, his death, as far as regards himself, cannot be reckoned premature, since he lived to finish the great work for which he seems to have been designed, and was rather removed from enjoyment than cut off from the acquisition of glory. How sincerely his loss was felt and lamented by those who had so long found their general security in his skill and conduct, and every consolation under their hardships in his tenderness and humanity, it is neither necessary nor possible for me to describe, much less shall I attempt to paint the horror with which we were struck, and the universal dejection and dismay which followed so dreadful and unexpected a calamity."

In commenting on Captain Cook's services, the same gentleman says:

"Perhaps no science ever received greater additions from the labours of a single man than geography has done from those of Captain Cook. In his first voyage to the South Seas he discovered the Society Islands; determined the insularity of New Zealand, discovered the Straits which separate the two islands, and are called after his name, and made a complete survey of both. He afterwards explored the eastern coast of New Holland, hitherto unknown, to an extent of twenty-seven degrees of latitude, or upwards of two thousand miles." In succeeding years he settled the disputed point of the existence of a great southern continent traversing the ocean there between the latitudes of 40° and 70° in such a way as to show the impossibility of its existence, "unless near the pole, and beyond the reach of navigation." (We may be permitted, in these days of general advancement, mental and physical, to doubt whether any part of the globe is *absolutely* "beyond the reach of navigation!") He discovered also the islands of New Caledonia and Georgia, and the Sandwich Islands; explored the western coasts of North America into the frozen regions, and ascertained the proximity of the two great continents of Asia and America. In short, — to use the words of his biographer, which compress the nature and value of the great navigator's services into a small and easily comprehended point — "if we except the sea of Amur and the Japanese Archipelago, which still remain imperfectly known to Europeans, he has completed the hydrography of the habitable globe."

*   *   *

Captain Cook has passed away, and the generation of men, with those whom he benefited and those who slew him, has gone to its account, but the coral islands remain as they were of old, resplendent with the beautiful works of God, though not, *as of old*, marred so terribly by the diabolical devices of man. "Cannibal Islands" some of them still are, without doubt, but a large proportion of them have been saved from heathen darkness by the light of God's Truth as revealed in the Holy Bible, and many thousands of islanders — including the descendants of those who slew the great Captain of the last generation — have enrolled themselves under the banner of the "Captain of our salvation," and are now, through God's mercy, clothed and in their right mind.

THE END

www.ingramcontent.com/pod-product-compliance
Lightning Source LLC
Chambersburg PA
CBHW022047170626
46808CB00003B/1394